THE BALEFIRE NOVELLA COLLECTION

BOX SET

REGINA WELLING

ERIN LYNN

CONTENTS

A DARING GAME

ONE SPELL OF A NIGHT

SHOT TO SPELL

WHEN SPELL FREEZES OVER

VACATION FROM MURDER

WICKED GIFT OF THE WITCH

A DARING GAME

A FATE WEAVER NOVELLA

CHAPTER

ONE

No more blind dates. I know my mother meant well and that everyone has a soul mate—yeah, sure—but this guy was not mine. If I had to listen to one more minute of him jabbering on about his exciting work in the field of accountancy, my head would explode.

Don't get me wrong, Martin was a nice enough guy and not bad looking, either. Dark hair, eyes to match, and a pair of shoulders that really filled out a suit. Snappy dresser, good table manners. Intelligent. Killer smile, and he seemed interested in me. The man was undeniably a catch.

What was wrong with me? Any woman would be lucky to date a guy like him, and here I was, hiding in the bathroom, wishing it had a back door or a window to slink out of.

I checked my teeth in the mirror for the third time and knew I was stalling. Twenty more minutes and a chocolate souffle in the bargain—I could survive that. Right? Right.

When I leaned back, I noticed a hot pink business card tucked into the mirror frame. Footswept Matchmaking was picked out in gold letters above the slogan, *Get Swept Away,* with a little logo of a broom in a field of stars and the phone number.

Tempting, but no. There was no way I would break my new no-blind-dating rule two minutes after making it. Not happening. Leaving the card there, I returned to my table and to Martin, who launched right into another work-related story that even the fluffy chocolate dessert filled with delicate cream could not make less boring.

I managed to shave three minutes off the end of the date without choking on the souffle, and since my place was only a short walk from the restaurant, insisted that I see myself home. Blinking Christmas lights played red, blue, and green over Martin's face as he leaned in for a kiss that landed on my cheek when I turned my head at the last second—right before I practically ran down the block.

He was probably still standing there as I unlocked the door to my townhouse apartment, and I know I should have felt guilty for that, but I didn't. All I felt was relief. Relief and a driving need to shed the skin I showed to the outside world and become my true self.

The transformation started with a yank at the pins holding my auburn hair in a twist tight enough to make my scalp itch. I shook out the shoulder-length mass and finger-combed it into a wild tumble before trading my skirt and blouse for soft leggings and a slouchy sweater. Pumps landed on the closet floor to be replaced by knit elf slippers that hugged my legs up to mid-calf level. Their curled-up toes bounced against my shins with each step.

On my way back into the family room, I clicked the button on dancing Santa, did a little two-step to the tinny tune of Rockin' Around the Christmas Tree, which reminded me to plug in my lights. Friday night, a few days before Christmas, I was on vacation until after the first of the year.

I love parts of my job—mainly the actual teaching parts. For the most part, third-graders are among my favorite people on earth; full of wonder, willing to learn, and genuinely interesting. Their parents and the politics of teaching...those I don't always love.

The next two weeks were my time, and I planned to turn hermit myself indoors and dive into the world of Myanthia. While my laptop booted up, I added a few final pieces to my outfit; half a dozen rings made from heavy silver adorned my hands, and I slid a circlet onto my forehead that matched the one my avatar wore in the game. The weight of the cool metal helped me get into character and complete my transformation into Lady Dare, the rogue demon hunter, daughter of Lord Dare, The Usurper. It didn't escape my attention that I was rebelling even in my make-believe world. Yeah, I've got issues. So what.

Donning my headset, I logged into my account, where the first thing I saw was a notice that I had finally unlocked the ability to purchase Whispering Blades, a set of daggers embellished with pink rhine-stones and imbued with the ability to gain health points with every hit. I had to have them, so I grabbed my purse. If there was one rule my dad had burned into my head, it was not to store credit card information in online accounts. As I pulled out my wallet, a business card fluttered to the floor. Funny, I didn't remember picking up any cards lately.

Turning it over, I read the name on the front. Footswept Matchmaking. Okay, how did that get in there? A flock of butterflies took flight in my belly. Had someone been in my purse? I could swear I had it with me the entire time I was at the restaurant. I laid the card aside, paid for my digital purchase, and loaded up Kingdoms of Myanthia. I had just started on a quest and imagined the cold winter wind whipping through my flowing auburn hair as my mount galloped across the snow-covered countryside when a ping indicated a private chat message.

Greetings, Lady Dare. Art thou traveling this perilous road alone? Please accept my humble offer to accompany the Lady across Ogre's Tooth Bridge, *for I fear for thou safety shouldst thou travel alone.*

I couldn't help but grin as I responded. *Why, Sir Kelin, the Lady thinketh thou rather forward and is insulted at thou insinuation that she needeth assistance. Ogres, trolls, demons; she hath slain thousands and shall suffer no injury at the hands of such fiends!*

Certainly, it would have been better to have whipped around and ridden off on my white unicorn with my head held high. Still, as I turned to face the pixelated horizon and canter toward the bridge, three level 30 ogres spawned nearby and began to attack my level 23 character. I knew I shouldn't have come through Ogre's Pass without leveling up a few notches, but there was a plethora of blue wildflowers on the other side, and I needed them to make a batch of experience boost potion. Irony—the bane of my existence.

Sir Kelin drew his sword from its scabbard and darted toward the first troll, lopping his head off with one fell swoop and immediately whirling a fireball toward the second, who let out a roar and dropped, burning, to his knees before falling over dead. I reflexively hopped off my steed and took the third troll out with a few quick stabs of my new daggers. One hit from him had my health bar flashing dangerously low, so I selected a potion from my Available Items list and downed it quickly.

Another ding. *Methinks the lady doth protest too much!*

Thank you kindly, good sir. I clicked the icon that looked like a pair of headphones next to Kelin's message and spoke into my headset. "But it was completely unnecessary. I could have taken them." I crossed my arms in front of my chest like a petulant child but could feel my cheeks blushing crimson as I heard the husky chuckle on the other end of the line. During my mini temper tantrum, I couldn't help but notice that my eye wandered more than once to the little pink card sticking out of my wallet. Maybe I could find a real, live man to come to my rescue every once in a while. Not that I needed one, of course.

If I was lucky, he would sound a bit like Sir Kelin's

voice in my headset. Something about his tone always cheered me up.

"Let's go get those flowers; I'll hold off any more ogre attacks, and you can make an extra potion as a thank you." Sir Kelin suggested, and we trotted off across the bridge.

CHAPTER

TWO

A pox upon the person who came up with the ugly Christmas sweater theme for parties. My parents had embraced this bit of foolishness with a passion bordering on the fanatic. With a sigh, I sewed the final touch, a set of battery operated LED lights, onto the confection of knitted hideousness I planned to wear. The sweater, a cardigan, was a thrift store find and ugly to begin with, but I had taken it up a notch by adding miniature tree ornaments, bits of garland, and the lights. As ugly sweaters went, this one was sublime. I buttoned it on thinking what a shame it was no one would see the dress underneath, a pretty sheath in a shade of blue that flattered my coloring.

I'll admit to having taken the scenic route to where my parents lived on the outer edge of the suburbs. My detour took me halfway across town to Swansea, the street where Christmas lights go to shine. I parked two blocks away to take a leisurely stroll through the twinkling fantasy land. A plaque at the dead end of the street gave a short history of how the whole thing had begun when two sets of neighbors tried to one-up each other in the decorating department and eventually turned the rivalry into a cooperative venture. I dropped a few dollars into the donation box slated for a children's charity, and noticed a short note thanking some local sponsors for donating time and money to the project.

The second name from the top of the list was, you guessed it, Footswept Matchmaking. Turning on my heel, I marched back to my car, thinking the lights looked dimmer in this direction.

Mom greeted me with a hug that ended up requiring assistance to end when a strand of garland from her sweater concoction tried mating with my string lights. Through his laughter, my dad finally managed to get us apart, and give me a careful hug. He had on a reject from the Cosby collection with no embellishments added. That put him right out of the running. My brother and his wife managed to make their contributions to the contest look elegant, which annoyed me to no end, but left only my mother and me in contention for the box of chocolates that was this year's prize.

I felt bad about winning the title from her until she pinned me in a corner and said, "Martin is such a nice man, dear. What could it hurt to go on one more date with him?"

"There was no chemistry, Mom. At all." I heard the whine settle into my voice, despised myself for it, but still could not help turning into a recalcitrant teen in the face of my mother's gently reproving tone.

"Chemistry isn't everything."

Maybe not to her, but it meant something to me. My mother's next words sent my blood pressure soaring.

"There's a nice young man at your father's firm. Brandon something or other. He's new in town and single..." She trailed off suggestively.

"No. No more blind dates. I'll find someone on my own. Please, Mom. Just let it go."

"You work all day and play on your computer all night. Where do you plan to find someone? Online?" My mother wrinkled her nose in distaste. "You're young and you need to get out and enjoy life. Meet new people. It makes me sad to think of you being alone. I do worry, you know."

I knew she did, and that her only wish was for me to be happy. I sighed. "Can we just enjoy the party without focusing on my dating life? I promise, I'll go on a date this week if that will make you happy." I lied. Right to her face.

Clearly it would, given the beaming smile she turned on me. "You've met someone? Tell me everything. What's he like?"

"I haven't met him yet," the lie grew deeper. "He's a friend of a friend," and was rewarded with a hug.

"Call me when it's over and tell me all about him." My brother called to Mom, who left me standing there feeling like the world's worst daughter. There was no man, no prospect for a date, and now I felt compelled to make it right. Shoulders hunched, I thrust my hands into the pockets of my ugly sweater. By now, it didn't even surprise me when my right hand encountered the stiff rectangle. I pulled out the business card and looked at the name fate seemed to be throwing in my face. Footswept Matchmaking. Taking my cell phone into the relative quiet of my parent's bedroom, I made the call. Hey, I know when I'm licked.

***By the time I was dressed for my interview with Lexi Balefire, my bedroom looked like the closet had thrown up. Half my clothes shrieked third grade teacher and the other half was a collection of gamer-geek-chic. Ripped jeans, patterned leggings, graphic tee after graphic tee, and a plethora of boots in various heights and colors were still relatively tame in comparison to the vast array of accessories I used to complete my look.

Who did I want to be today? That was a question I struggled with all the time. My closet offered no middle ground—hence the current level of chaos as a result of trying to find a way to blend the two sides of my personality into one cohesive look. In the end, I shrugged on a work outfit and pledged to ponder the existential ramifications of the mess while I cleaned it up later.

I walked into Footswept Matchmaking expecting to meet a middle aged woman with hair teased up to there, and a heavily-accented, gravelly voice. I couldn't have been more surprised to meet Lexi, a woman around my own age with a pert nose and shining eyes. My expectations shifted. She would pull out a computer, ask a million questions, and run my profile through some kind of matching software.

None of that happened. In fact, after we signed an agreement and I put my sorely abused credit card back in my purse, she barely prodded me to talk, and then I couldn't seem to stop myself.

"Tell me a little bit about yourself." Lexi flipped a lock of sable hair over one ear and fixed interested eyes on mine. We drifted toward a pair of stuffed armchairs covered in bold geometric patterns, and before I knew what was happening, I was spilling my guts. It was like she'd cast a truth spell over me.

I explained how straitlaced my parents were; why I chose teaching out of all the other possibilities in order to satisfy their expectations; their hope for me to marry someone who looked good on paper. And then I launched right into what I imagined in a man. "He has to share my love for fantasy; but also be able to get through a Tolstoy novel. He has to be tough enough to protect me; but also know when to let me stand up for myself. He has to be romantic; but not a crybaby. He has to know how to let loose and have some fun; but he also needs to be a responsible adult and get along with my family. And he has to accept me for all my quirkiness, and love that I'm a dorky gamer chick who bakes Legend of Zelda cupcakes on the weekends." I nearly choked on my verbal incontinence. What had possessed me to tell things to a total stranger that I had never even spoken out loud?

Lexi's ruby red lips parted in a smile, one perfectly-groomed eyebrow arched conspiratorially. "So you want the best of both worlds—that's us women for you. We're all a little bit like Goldilocks. Fortunately, it's all relative, and there's a perfect match out there just waiting for you." She rolled her eyes during the last bit and then rose to her feet. "I promise, that's the last time I'll say the phrase *perfect match*. I know it sounds like the name of an online dating site. Trust me, I have a magical touch."

"Are we done?" I wasn't sure if I was expected to stand also, so I did, shifting my weight from foot to foot while Lexi examined me from head to toe. Shouldn't there be more to it than that?

"No, we're just getting started. I hope you don't have plans, because we're going on an adventure. But we've got to work on your outfit. You can't go where we're going looking like that."

I wasn't sure whether to be offended or not, but as I looked down at the demure neckline of my plain Jane A-line dress and cardigan sweater I squirmed a little. Still, it took some kind of guts to just tell a client they needed a makeover. And where could we possibly be going? She had just met me 20 minutes ago. Apparently

Lexi noticed my momentary pause, because her eyes and tone softened.

"You look just like a third grade teacher should; but it's clear that you're not completely comfortable. This," She waved a dainty finger at me, "is only half the story. Am I wrong?" She crossed her arms and arched that eyebrow again, daring me to disagree. It was a gesture expected of a close friend, not someone you had just met, but somehow I had a feeling that Lexi Balefire could get away with just about anything she wanted to.

"Come with me." She commanded gently, leading me to a door across the office I had assumed was the restroom. It turned out to be Barbie's Dream Closet, and I couldn't help but gasp as we walked through a short hallway lined with hooks that held a rainbow of scarves, hats, belts, and handbags in styles ranging from Vogue to Good Housekeeping. The room beyond was bigger than the office out front by at least a factor of two; it looked like the inside of a Macy's fitting room on Christmas Eve on one side, and a miniature salon on the other. An oversize glamour shot of one of the best-looking men I had ever seen took up nearly the entire wall above the gleaming chrome barber's chair.

"Who's that?" I asked, nodding at the blond Adonis.

Lexi grinned. "That's Wyn, my business partner, for all intents and purposes. He's the best stylist I've ever seen, but he's on a cruise ship somewhere in the Caribbean right now, so we're on our own. Gorgeous, though, isn't he?

Fifteen minutes later I found myself sitting cross-legged on the floor, surrounded by dozens of articles of clothing and wishing I could just stuff them in my bag and bolt. But that would be rude, and with my luck I'd wind up on the nightly news under the "Stupid Criminals" heading. I ended up in a red plaid tailored shirtdress cinched around my waist by a rhinestone-studded black belt and knee-high black suede boots that somehow managed to look appropriate and sexy at the same time, a chunky necklace in gunmetal gray gleaming around my neck. Once Lexi had deftly curled my hair into beachy waves using a behemoth-sized triple-barrel iron, I applied a coat of black mascara and achieved a cat eye look with a particularly user-friendly curved eyeliner pen. A thin coat of lip gloss made my lips shimmer subtly, and we were off. Not that I had any idea where we were off *to*.

Winding her arm in mine, Lexi practically dragged me down the street. I kept glancing at her out of the corner of my eye because she seemed to be walking aimlessly, yet with a purpose. I know that's an oxymoron, but that's the best way to describe her pace. Little winged dollar signs danced before my eyes. Lexi's services didn't come cheap, and for the kind of money this was costing me, I wanted something a bit more professional.

Lexi stopped and gazed toward an establishment called The Grind with a curious smile on her face. Through the window I could see men and women in business suits sipping lattes out of enormous cups. "In here."

"No," I balked at the door. "This is exactly the kind of place where the man of my mother's dreams would hang out. Isn't there somewhere else we should be?"

"Trust me." Lexi insisted. I didn't, but I let her drag me inside anyway.

The place looked like any other upscale coffee bar. Round tables, leather seating, lots of polished nickel accents. I hated these places with a passion. Lexi paused in the doorway radiating the feral intensity of a wolf scenting prey. That lasted only a few seconds before she had me by the arm again, and was dragging me toward the bored-looking Barista standing behind the gleaming counter. Distracted by the size of the menu lining the upper part of the back wall, I wasn't prepared for what Lexi did next.

As we walked past one of the tables, I swear Lexi gave me a hard shove with her elbow. My feet tangled against each other and I landed hard in the lap of a man using his computer. He caught me with one hand and slammed the laptop closed with the other to keep me from seeing what he had been working on. Not that I cared about that, anyway. My face flamed and I apologized while I struggled to get off of him. "I'm sorry. So sorry. I'm not usually this clumsy." I shot a look at Lexi over his shoulder and got back an unrepentant grin.

The face looking down at mine wasn't quite as close to perfection as the one hanging in Lexi's hidden salon, but it was close. Chiseled jaw, dark chocolate eyes with an amused glint in them, and lips that looked warm and inviting. He was the whole package. Well, except for the corporate suit and the tie nestled under a chin with a cute little cleft that made me want to lay a finger just there.

I realized he was cradling me in his arms and that I had been staring at him a moment too long. My face heated again and I renewed my efforts to rise.

"It's not every day a beautiful woman just falls into my lap." The man, still holding me firmly, stood and set me gently back on my feet with minimal effort. I'm no Amazon, but I'm not a waif, either. There was untapped strength under all that business attire. "The fates must be smiling on me today." He brushed a few stray crumbs from my arm. Apparently on the way down, I had smashed his chocolate crunch donut.

"I'm Brandon Kelly."

"Felicity Dare. Sorry about your donut."

"Make it up to me by letting me take you to dinner."

His logic was flawed on that one. I opened my mouth to say no when Lexi answered for me. "She'd love to."

Back outside, I rounded on her, "What were you thinking? You just made a date for me with corporate Ken. He's everything I don't want in a man. Weren't you listening at all?"

"Trust me."

"Trust you? I don't even know you! And you definitely don't know me." Forget about the part where she had hand-picked the perfect outfit—and in my size, no less.

Lexi sighed and yanked me down the street a touch too roughly for someone I was paying a service fee, but I fell into step beside her with a terse, "Where are we going now?"

"You'll see."

We marched down three blocks and took two sharp

turns to the left, bringing us to the back side of a two-story warehouse-style building that appeared deserted save for a blinking neon light that, upon further inspection was actually a laser beam tracing the letters "p2p" at high speed. Puzzled, I looked at Lexi, who was now wearing a wide grin.

"You've never been here, have you?" She asked.

"No." I breathed, my spidey senses tingling. In gamer-speak, p2p was an acronym for "pay to play", referring to a game that charged a monthly fee. That could only mean one thing: this was some kind of gaming establishment. Of course I had heard of such places; but mostly from friends who played in foreign countries—they're not as common here in the States. All thoughts of meeting my soul mate went out the window as curiosity overwhelmed my senses.

Lexi yanked open the door, spilling a rainbow of light onto the pavement at our feet. A large white arrow glowed in the glare of a black light bulb, and directed us through a hallway twinkling with multicolored strobe lights and toward a tall counter manned by a young woman with a bright blue pixie hairstyle. She wore a black t-shirt printed with an old original Nintendo controller over a denim miniskirt, and her arms and hands were covered with dozens of bracelets and rings.

Lexi sidestepped the counter and veered left into the crowd.

I looked around, taking in the rows of computer stations filled with intense-looking gamers wearing headsets and clicking away furiously on games ranging across several genres from fantasy, to real-time strategy, to first-person shooter. Booths lined the outer edge of the space on elevated platforms, and I was surprised to see a waitress on roller skates zoom through the masses to deliver a steaming basket of fries. On further inspection, they weren't traditional roller skates, but rather a pair of those sneakers with the wheels that popped out of the soles.

A banner strung across the rafters caught my attention and I pointed excitedly to Lexi. "Kingdoms of Myanthia, that's my game! There's a gathering here next weekend. Look, you get free admission if you cosplay—that means come in costume—and they're organizing a multi-player quest for anyone who logs in from the p2p server!" I rambled on while Lexi dragged me forward.

We settled into a table in the far corner; the best vantage point in the place, and Lexi ordered us drinks while I ogled computer screens to see what everyone was playing. When the waitress returned and handed me a vanilla coke with a lemon slice—a concoction of my own making—I shot a puzzled look at Lexi, who deftly ignored it and began pointing around the room.

"So do you see Mr. Right anywhere?" She asked quietly.

Once again I surveyed the room, this time looking at the people rather than the games on their screens. As a place to meet like-minded people, this was Nirvana and Utopia all rolled into one. From a dating perspective, it was a frog parade. Who knew so many men in their fifties liked gaming? Aside from them, the vast majority belonged to the barely-old-enough-to-legally-drink crowd, and most of the rest of the room fell into the undateable category. In fact, my only age-appropriate option was a man wearing vintage gray sweat pants. You know, the kind with the elastic gathering at the ankles. Eyes glazed from hours of screen time peered fixedly forward while he worked the keyboard and mouse with feverish passion, which might have been better spent wielding a razor. Stubble can be sexy—three day old scruff meant it had probably been that long since he'd been acquainted with soap or water. Nope. Just nope.

If this was all Lexi had up her sleeve, I'd be making use of her money back guarantee. Still, I had technically fulfilled the promise to my mother. I was going on a date this week even if I wasn't happy about it.

I snuggled into a pair of fleece-lined leggings printed with strings of Christmas lights, a Rudolph sweatshirt complete with light-up nose, and a fuzzy green and red striped robe. Tiny Santa Clauses dripped from my earlobes and I had replaced my circlet with a reindeer antler headband. As I pulled on an elf slipper my eyes were drawn to the discarded pair of boots I had borrowed from Lexi's closet and decided that after tonight's experience, she probably wasn't getting them back. They were just too pretty.

Myanthia was decorated for the holiday season, the towns littered with snowmen, twinkle lights, and festive wreaths. A quick look at my friends list indicated that Sir Kelin was online, and a moment later a message pinged into a private chat window.

Greetings, My Lady. How art though this evening?

Well and good, kind Sir. Yourself?

Tis one thing only I lack in life milady. If thou wouldst grant me the boon of knowing your true name, my quest would be complete.

My mind went immediately to Mr. Sweatpants from p2p. Pass.

Let us not complicate the quest, Sir Kelin. Art thou ready to enter the fray?

Shall I tell thee my own true name first?

I dropped the game speak. *I prefer to keep my real life separate from my gaming one. It's a choice I made a long time ago, and I hope it won't interfere with our friendship in the game. Do you understand?*

There was a short pause.

Of course, my lady. Whatever you wish.

I hoped that would not be the end of our communication, but I meant to stand my ground. Another pause lengthened before more words appeared in the window.

Hast thou daggers at the ready? Onward into the fight.

And we played.

CHAPTER
THREE

Trading one of my all-day gaming marathons for a dinner date with a buttoned-up desk jockey. How had I gotten roped into this? If my dating history was anything to go by, I knew exactly how this would go. He'd show up in one of two types of vehicles. A gas-saving car the size of an overgrown golf cart or one of those ubiquitous sedans with nothing but numbers for a name. Then, depending on which vehicle he was driving, I could count of one of two types of restaurants. It would be a flow chart of a date. Golf cart car equaled Italian restaurant—sedan big enough that he was probably compensating meant we would be eating French food. It never failed.

Taking Lexi's advice, out of all the offerings in my closet, I chose one of the dresses that spoke to Lady Dare. Forest green with gold braided trim on the sleeves, a tightly fitted bodice, and a skirt that draped softly to mid-calf. The dress paired perfectly with gold ballet flats.

I wasn't expecting my heart to skip a beat when the doorbell rang. Or for it to speed up at the sight of Brandon's smiling face. Okay, so he was attractive enough to get my juices flowing, but that didn't make him my type. Then again, it seemed my type only existed in computer games.

"I hope you don't mind if we go someplace a little different for dinner. There's this new place that opened up over on Winchester Street and I've been hearing really good things." Brandon helped me into his pickup truck.

"You mean the Bard and Grill?" Maybe this guy had a little more going for him than I'd thought. The Bard and Grill was a brand new steakhouse with a Medieval theme. Judging by the gallery on their website, it was the kind of place Lady Dare and Sir Kelin would go to enjoy a night of feasting and fun. Too bad I was stuck going there with Corporate Ken instead. I turned sideways in my seat to squint at him appraisingly. He couldn't have known I was dying to check the place out, could he?

When I didn't answer right away he said, "Is that a dumb idea? Maybe you'd rather have Italian or French."

I'll admit my snort was less than ladylike, but it

loosened up something inside me. Something that reared up and dared me to give the guy a chance—to plumb his hidden depths, and maybe even let him plumb mine. My inner voice has a dirty mind sometimes.

"Absolutely not. Take me to the Bard and Grill kind sir."

I gave him a smile and in return, Brandon squeezed my hand. I watched his hands as he put the truck into gear. His long fingers sent delicious tingles running over me from the point of contact, and I couldn't remember the last time a man made me feel this way with nothing more than a touch.

Bard and Grill lived up to my expectations in every way. Walking through the door felt like stepping into a scene from Myanthia. Rustic tables made from thickly planked wood, a roaring fire in the centrally located fireplace, and half-timbered walls all lent to the feel of a wayside pub right out of the game. Beside me, Brandon seemed just as mesmerized as I was.

A waitress, kitted out in her best serving wench attire, led us to a cozy table near the fire and the date moved up another level when Brandon's hand resting on the small of my back sent shivers up my spine.

During appetizers, we talked about everything—work, family, and favorite childhood books.

"Grimm or Andersen?" He asked.

"Both. Totally. I always loved the story of Elsa and the swan brothers. I remember visiting my grandmother when I was eight, maybe nine, and falling into a patch of nettles out at the farm. I was a total mess, and my grandmother gave me that story to read." My eyes burned with unshed tears. "She loved books, everything about them. I've tried to pass that on to my students because I know it would make her proud."

This was not a first date conversation, but I felt comfortable talking to Brandon. Not in a brotherly kind of way, but in that I've-just-met-you-but-I-feel-like-I've-known-you-forever way.

"It was my uncle for me. He read everything he could get his hands on—and I mean everything. Westerns to romance. Every birthday or holiday he gave me a new a book or two, and he always read them first so we could talk about them later. According to him, every story could be traced back to a fairy tale, and it was our private game to trace all his gifts back to their origins. He hated the tweaked Disney versions, though."

"Right? Where every story has a happy ending and the characters all live in a pink and blue pastel world. Life is more like the originals, where instead of happily ever after, it was—hey, we survived, but it was a close thing and messy besides."

Some dark memory painted lines of tension around Brandon's mouth, stole a bit of the brilliance from his smile, but before I could ask him about it, sizzling, butter-drenched steaks appeared before us and we got distracted.

Mine was so tender it practically jumped into bits at the sight of my knife. I took the first bite and nearly moaned in pleasure, "My arteries are seizing up already, but it's totally worth it."

"Really good." Brandon's enthusiasm was a pale, flaccid thing—way less than the steaks deserved. I cast my mind back to the conversation right before the food showed up, and felt comfortable enough to ask him outright. "Want to tell me about it?"

"About what?"

"Come on. Something touched a nerve."

"Isn't there a rule against discussing romantic histories on a first date?"

And there it was. You know what I mean. You're on a

date and it's going really well, so well you get to thinking this might actually go somewhere and then—BAM! There it is. The thing that puts the brakes on and makes you realize why this person is still single. Getting maudlin about your ex is right up there on the list of date killers. It's either just before or just after talking about how the only person who understands you is your cat. Or your dog. Or, God forbid, your mother.

But darned if I wasn't curious what his story was. "You have to tell me now, or I'll make up something worse in my head." I kept my tone intentionally light and smiled at him over a bite of roasted squash.

He blushed. Just the faintest hint of pink, but still. "I was in a long-term relationship. I proposed, and instead of saying yes, she explained how just about everything about me would need to change if we were going to stay together. I decided she wasn't worth it and walked away."

Nice. I'd been prattling on about happily ever after, and he had this in his past. I'm sorry sounded trite, so I countered with my own sordid tale. "I've been on seventeen first dates this year—all arranged by my parents—and zero second ones. My confession brought the merest hint of a smile. "According to my mother, I'm consigning her to a life barren of grandchildren."

Brandon leaned back in his chair and eyed me spec-ulatively. "I think our mothers might hit it off. They seem to sing the same tunes."

I suppose it might be considered brazen, but given the spark I felt sizzling between us, I thought I deserved to know if he was hung up on his ex before I wasted a second date on him. Yeah, I was thinking about breaking my streak. Epic, right? Most of my romantic experiences have been lived out in fiction, and I've read enough books where I thought the heroine was an idiot for making assumptions, so I asked him right out. "Are you still in rebound mode?"

After a split second of shock, my question was rewarded by a rich laugh that evoked a mental image of Sir Kelin for some reason.

"Go out with me again and find out."

A short but furious battle raged in my mind. My mother would love this man, and part of me wanted to reject him for that reason alone, but I felt a pull toward him that was impossible to define or deny.

"Okay."

Outside my townhouse, I had just stepped onto the sidewalk when someone jostled me from behind and knocked me hard into side of the truck.

"Oh, sorry." A teenage boy who lived a few buildings down from mine looked up from his phone. "Sorry, Miz Dare. I wasn't looking where I was going. There's a Bulbasaur around here somewhere." He grinned up at me and showed me his screen.

Another victim of the craze.

"It's okay. No harm done. Just look up a little more often from now on, all right? And check over there," I pointed toward the mailbox at the end of the street. "That's where I found him once." The boy went on his way and that was when I noticed Brandon's surprised expression.

"Pokemon Go, huh?"

Before I had a chance to decide whether he was judging me or just making a comment, he had gathered me into his arms and his lips were deliciously close to mine. I leaned in to close the gap and every thought drained out of my head except for how right, how good this felt. Brandon's lips were warm against mine. Soft and firm at the same time. The kiss shot through me to curl my toes—after a few stops at some other places along the way.

For the length of the kiss, a hundred Pokemon could have danced a jig beside me and I wouldn't have noticed. I never wanted it to end.

It did end, though. It ended as softly as it began,

and with Brandon resting his forehead lightly against mine.

"Tomorrow night. I'll pick you up at seven." His voice sounded breathless and I only nodded, then fumbled my way inside.

CHAPTER

FOUR

I shut the door and leaned back against it, a stupidly content smile on my face, eyes closed, replaying the moment in my mind just like in the romantic comedies I'd outwardly mocked and secretly adored my whole life. Brandon's husky voice as he leaned in, the cool scent of his breath, and the softness of his lips; I sighed and opened my eyes lazily. Then my senses came back into focus as my gaze lit on my computer desk across the room.

Brandon's tone when he made that crack about my Pokemon game caused a sick, uneasy feeling to form in the pit of my stomach. Just when I was starting to think that maybe he wasn't the square I assumed he was when I fell into his lap at The Grind; with that one comment I was suddenly unsure. A little voice inside my head that sounded suspiciously like Lexi Balefire whispered *Yeah, silly, but then he kissed you.*

That was true, but maybe he just wanted to see if I'd

invite him in for a nightcap or some other ridiculous excuse for sex. *Did he seem like that kind of guy to you?* The voice intoned. Well, not really, but you never knew anymore. Sometimes it was the nicest guys who tried to get into your pants on the first date.

So what if he was a great kisser and read fairy tales. My life fit right into the story of Beauty and the Beast—only, I was the beast who presented two faces to the world. Mild-mannered school teacher by day, rabid gaming geek chick by night. Brandon couldn't be my beauty if he couldn't accept my beast.

Mind made up, I pulled my phone out of my purse and searched for the number Brandon had entered into it earlier. My finger hesitated over the dial icon, but I'm ashamed to say, I took the coward's way out by hitting the messaging icon instead.

About tomorrow night, I can't make it after all. I'm sorry—Felicity

Hitting send, I didn't even wait for the telltale ping that signaled a sent message before jamming my phone back into my purse and stuffing that into the closet. Whatever answer Brandon might return would have to wait until tomorrow. For now, I needed to visit the one place where sorrow could never touch me, Myanthia.

I flicked on my computer, contemplating the evening some more, and had just opened Kingdoms of Myanthia when an update screen popped up: Crucial Update Required. Please Close All Programs Until Update Is Complete.

Wonderful. I watched the progress bar crawl slowly up to 9% and then waited a solid five minutes before I couldn't take it anymore. I decided to kill some time and began bedecking myself with rhinestone costume jewelry and getting into Lady Dare mode. I was already wearing the dress, and I needed to lose myself while I sorted out my feelings.

I peeked at my computer again; mercifully, the update was complete and I was able to log in with no further issues. Ping. I smiled and donned my headset, flicking the microphone on as I did, and heard Sir Kelin's voice floating across the wire. The connection wasn't perfect; static crackled on the line, but it was a peak usage hour so that was probably as good as it was going to get.

"Fast travel to Stonewall, quick. I'm in the middle of this Gorum fight and it's only got 20% health. If you assist you'll get a shard bonus, and I know you need those for your Ultima."

Alrighty then. All business tonight. What happened

to my sweet, chivalrous knight? I waited to load into Stonewall and met Kelin at the fight.

"Oh, good, you made it." He sounded cheerful, but not nearly as flirtatious as usual.

I pulled Lady Dare's bow from its quiver and aimed for the Gorum beast's head, hitting him square in between the eyes and draining his health down to zero. "There, he's dead. You're welcome."

Kelin laughed. "Thanks for that last hit; the four of us have only been fighting him for fifteen minutes, but it's all you." He teased.

"You know it! So how was your day?" I asked, keeping my tone light and conversational. Static made his answer unintelligible, and when it cleared the blood drained from my face. "...went on a date for the first time in a long time."

It hit me harder than it should have. I had somehow pinned my hopes on this fictional knight, and he wasn't even real. I struggled to maintain calm as I spoke. "Oh, good for you. Did you have a good time?"

"Actually, I really did. It was fun; I think we're going to go out again. Ooh, there's another team fight going on over by the Emerald Forest. Want to see if we can pick up some more shards?" Kelin's character disappeared from the screen, and I clicked the Fast Travel button to follow him.

I ran back over our past conversations in my head. Sure, he had been a bit flirty, and had asked for my name on more than one occasion, but had he ever said anything more blatant? Now that I really thought about it, he hadn't. Most of our banter was in period speak, just role playing as Lady Dare and Sir Kelin. I knew nothing about this guy, and yet I had built him up on a pedestal just because his character was the perfect fantasy man.

And what was I getting jealous over, anyway? Not much more than an hour ago, I kissed a man who made my knees go weak and who had surprised me more in one date than any of the other seventeen losers I had met this year.

For the first time ever, I shut the game off without saving my progress. With furious motions, I stripped off the bits and pieces of Lady Dare—the rings landed on the dresser with a clink, and the dress sailed across the room to land in a heap on the chair. I brushed my teeth so hard they bled, and then climbed into bed where I tossed and turned for hours.

It all played through my head like a video documentary. See Felicity run. From one bad date to another.

Always looking for the Knight of her dreams. Watch as she shot down one perfectly good man after another who didn't live up to her ideal.

And that's when it hit me like a ton of bricks. I was holding all of these blind dates to the Sir Kelin standard; had been even before I started playing with Sir Kelin. I was in love with the idea of him, and not the reality that any other man could provide. I had been a fool. A blind, stubborn fool.

It must have been close to daybreak when I finally fell off the cliff of exhaustion and into a deep, but troubled sleep. Consequently, it was close to noon before I dragged my eyes open again. Hurray for vacation.

Half an hour later, with a mug of coffee in my hand, I dug my phone out and laid it on the table with about the same amount of care as I would have if it had been a snake. Right now, that bit of plastic, metal, and silicon was my worst enemy. I knew it was probably too late to call Brandon and make it right, but I had to try.

Taking a deep breath, I picked up the torture device and dialed Brandon's number. I cringed as it belted out its fifth ring, and when I heard the recorded message instructing me to "leave it at the beep", I hung up, embarrassed and relieved he hadn't answered.

What if he was screening? Now I was picturing him

hitting the ignore icon, and wasn't that great for my limited self-esteem?

The only thing left to do was call Lexi. I pulled up her number, but before I could hit the send button, my calendar app chimed to remind me that the Myanthia gathering started in a few hours. Savagely, I hit the dismiss button. No way. I was not in the mood today. Maybe there would be another one in a month or two.

Five minutes later, the calendar app chimed again. Myanthia Gathering. Dismiss.

Lexi answered on the first ring. That was odd, no one ever does that.

"I hope you have some other options ready, because I blew the date with Brandon." I didn't even bother with hello when I snarled into the phone. "I told you he was the wrong man for me."

Lexi's voice, full of calm and reason, soothed when she said, "Trust me, Felicity. It will all work out. Go to your Myanthia party and have a good time. I promise it's going to be fine. I know you think you'd rather stay home and lick your wounds, but it will do you good to get out and these things don't happen every day."

I grumbled a bit, and got off the phone. Lexi was right, though, this would be my only chance to attend a similar function. Once the newness wore off, avid

Myanthians would keep playing, but p2p would have moved on to the next gaming fad. Besides, hanging around with my peers might improve my mood. If I wanted free admission, I'd better get cleaned up and put together a costume.

Red this time. A dress similar to the green I'd worn to my date with Brandon, only this one took things up a notch. I braided my hair to frame my favorite circlet, and used makeup to cover the pale sleeplessness on my face. Silver rings and ballet flats completed the look. My stomach felt hollow as I made my way to p2p.

The place was packed with characters right out of the game. Even sweat pants guy was there. In his sweat pants naturally, but he'd added a tee shirt painted to look like armor and a helmet made out of cardboard and duct tape. Looking around the room, I saw several actual suits of armor. What can I say? We gamers take these things seriously. There was only one person seated near the back of the room who had declined to dress up. I couldn't see a face under the shadowed brim of a ball cap, but I remember thinking there was one in every crowd.

Declining to join any of the groups, I made my way to one of the computers, swiped my card through the reader, donned a headset, and logged in. Sir Kelin's voice came over the line almost as soon as I popped into the game.

"Well met, Lady Dare."

"Greetings, Sir Kelin. What shall we quest for today?" He sounded subdued.

"Do you mind if I ask you a question? You know, about women."

"Well, I can't speak for the general population, but go ahead."

"What would make a woman just change her mind? I mean, I thought the date went well. We had a connection, you know—and she just...we were supposed to see each other again and she changed her mind."

Okay, this was spooky. Sir Kelin could be anywhere in the world—this was the Internet age, after all—and we were having the same basic experience in our dating life. At exactly the same time.

"Maybe she got the impression you didn't share her interests." I projected my experience with Brandon onto him and it all got away from me. "So what if I play stupid games online. So what if I like to chase Pokemon in my spare time. Why can't anyone accept me for who I am? A gamer geek." The rant was out of place, but I couldn't seem to shut up.

I heard a pause. A palpable one.

"From one gamer geek to another, Pokemon Go can be dangerous. People don't always look where they're going when they're playing, and there are stories of people who have been hurt. It's a great game in theory, but in practice, it has its downsides. Felicity? Is that you?"

My body turned into the equivalent of a jumping bean playground. Have you ever had that feeling when your heart tries to leap at the same time your stomach tries to drop? Was it possible that Brandon and Sir Kelin were the same person?

"Brandon?"

"Why did you...what happened? I thought we had something good going."

"I had a stupid moment, I guess. Can you forgive me?"

"Only if you'll keep our date."

"Of course I will." He was supposed to pick me up in fifteen minutes, so I'd better get myself home. "Let me just go get ready." I whipped off the headset and jumped out of my seat.

Across the room, I saw a man dressed as Sir Kelin stand and our eyes met. My knight in the game and in real life crossed the space between us and pulled me into his arms.

Over his shoulder, a sudden movement caught my eye. The woman wearing the ball cap tipped up her head so I could see her face. Lexi Balefire winked at me as though she had known this would happen all along. Who knows, maybe she had. Brandon swallowed my quiet laugh as his lips claimed mine.

ONE SPELL OF A NIGHT
A FATE WEAVER NOVELLA

ONE

Any other day, it might be disturbing to open my front door and face a band of hungry monsters, ghosts, and vampires. If they weren't joined by Pikachu and the Mario Brothers, that is.

I might even be inclined to pelt them with flaming arrows or shoot sparks out of my fingertips, but today the acceptable response was to ply the little beasties with Snickers and Reese's Peanut Butter Cups.

Except it was only 4:30 and all of the Reese's were already gone. I'd like to say I handed them out to the children, but the chocolate stain on my orange and black striped tights proved otherwise.

Yes, I know it's not very original for a real witch to don a pointy hat and shoes for Halloween. I also believe my sister witches might strap me to a stake as punishment for the green face paint and hooked latex nose, but my sense of humor tends toward sarcasm and puns. Besides, I was totally alone in the house—

save for my familiar, Salem, and his new crush, Pyewacket—so there were no faerie godmothers or grandmothers or great aunts around to weigh in on my choices.

As if the mere act of thinking about him had called Salem forth, he streaked down the stairs on four legs and transformed into his human form in a flurry of jet-black fur.

"The Grinch and Cindy Lou Who? Interesting choice."

"What? Too cutesy?"

"No. Just right." And if they made it out the door in the next ten seconds, I might be able to hold back the laugh threatening to burst free.

Salem knows me too well, one blue and one green eye narrowed as he detected the twinkle in mine.

"Hah!" Pyewacket, all lush curves, and mysterious eyes missed the wide-eyed innocent look by a mile. "I told you. Now we go with my choice." Her entire body shivered, and when she was done, She Ra stood before me in all her superhero glory. The winged headdress held back a fall of blond hair that set off her bronzed skin perfectly. Under the white tunic, her legs went on for miles before disappearing into a pair of gold boots.

"Come on," she poked a reluctant Salem in the ribs.

"We're not going as The Grinch and She Ra. That would be creepy."

"This is the worst. Why can't we go as Mickey and Minnie? At least that would be funny for a reason." A miniature tornado of dark fur resolved into He-Man. Salem tossed a lock of blond hair behind one ear and looked down at himself in disgust. "I'm wearing a brown diaper with knee-length boots and what is this thing supposed to be?" He tugged at the sword sheath that fell in an X shape across his chest.

"Well, I think you look hot." Pyewacket winked at me, and I knew poor Salem was sunk. "Let's go save the universe."

"You're leaving me here to hand out candy all by myself?" I teased, secretly thrilled for an evening that didn't necessitate a sound-dampening spell to drown out the strangely intimate purring noises coming from Salem's temporary room in the attic. So many icks.

"I'm sure you'll be fine on your own. If I miss another one of Pepper's fabulous parties, I won't get invited back—besides, Cobweb Bones is playing a private set for us, and I'm dying to see them." He responded, refusing to meet my gaze full on.

"You just want to show off your hot new girlfriend to all your familiar buddies, don't lie," I whispered out of the corner of my mouth. "Have fun." I'd thought Salem a confirmed bachelor, but it seemed Pye's—ahem—charms were enough to coax him out of early retirement.

The doorbell pealed again as the next group of sugar-shocked children clamored for more free candy, and I hurried to the foyer with a skip in my step.

I'll tell you a little secret, though I doubt it will come as much of a surprise: I love Halloween. Not Samhain, the festival of the dead we witches consider akin to New Year's Eve, though I do enjoy ushering the sun God to sleep and welcoming the onset of the winter season.

I swear if you tell any of the members of my coven that I can be found walking like an Egyptian to The Monster Mash every October 31, I'll hex you with a case of witch pox so quickly it will make your head spin.

Truthfully, I'd rather stay at home handing out candy than brave the streets of Port Harbor on the night when the veil between the living and the dead is thinnest. I might be a witch, and I'm even part God—my Dad's Cupid, the antithesis of The Great Pumpkin, no less—but ghosts and dead people still freak me out.

From upstairs, I heard a banging noise, similar to someone clinking a wrench against a pipe, or the noise a radiator makes when it fires up. Except we don't have radiators in the Balefire house; we have a magical fire that not only feeds the magic of all witchkind but renders any other source of heat unnecessary and redundant.

"Salem?" I called. "Did you forget something?" Maybe he climbed up the drain pipe and crawled into the attic window to avoid yet another cluster of kids congregating on the front porch.

"Hello, little children," I cackled, playing my part to a T while keeping one ear open in case Salem decided to sneak up behind me and pull a little Halloween prank of his own and dropped candy into the bags of an entire family of Minions. So cute.

More banging and clinking erupted from the area behind the parlor.

"Salem?" I yelled again.

He wouldn't be foolish enough to go into the workshop when there were so many straights around. All we needed was for some curious kid to see him reach into the raging Balefire flames and pull the handle that opened the access door behind the fireplace.

If he wasn't in the workshop, that only left one other place.

No way he'd ventured into the faerie godmothers'

wing without permission, whether they were home or not. Heck, I hardly ever went in there, and I wasn't the one who'd been perma-banned for dripping tuna salad on their sitting room sofa. Knowing the faeries, they could slap him with a mouthful of rotten fish as punishment, even from halfway across the country. My faerie godmothers tended to toss magic around first and ask questions never.

"If you're trying to scare me, it's not working." I lied through my teeth and received no response. If it wasn't Salem, could someone else have gotten into the house?

I set the bowl of candy on the front porch, slapped a quick charm on it to ensure none of the greedy little goblins would get away with more than one piece each, and locked the door behind me. A flick of the finger made every curtain in the house snap shut, and a dusk-like darkness fell around me.

I crept down the hall, one pointed shoe in front of the other and realized I hadn't taken into account tracking down—or running away from—a predator when considering my choice of footwear.

What sort of predator, I didn't know, but we'd had an eaflock, a demon, and a rabid Raythe in the house within the last six months or so, and it was anyone's guess what the next guest's bestial classification might be.

Don't ask why, but I grabbed for an umbrella from the coat rack in the hall and wound up with a handful of fake spider web before I realized if anyone charged me, I could just shoot them with the Bow of Destiny strapped to my proverbial back. Or, duh, use my magic. Just my luck I'd fire off an arrow and end up the new love interest of some wayward hellbeast. Not a great plan.

With squared shoulders and a smidgen more confidence, I swept the kitchen and entryway, then circled back through the parlor where the Balefire burned a festive orange, fading to black and finally purple in the center of the flame.

Lacking the Balefire blessing no one with half a brain would have dared reach into the flames for the handle that would open the fireplace into my secret sanctum, which meant the noise couldn't have come from in there. Unless...

There was one Balefire who definitely shouldn't be allowed into the room full of family secrets: my own mother, Sylvana. It would be just my luck, too, if she showed up while I was home alone. The woman had caused me no end of trouble in payment for a single favor. Granted, for a simple favor, it had been a major deal—passing on the Stone of Blood amulet I needed to complete my transition from neophyte to full-fledged witch.

With no idea what I would do if I found her there, I thrust my hand into the fire and waited for the door of the sanctum to creak open, took a deep breath, and stepped through.

Nothing was there. Baseless paranoia had me caught up in the spirit of the holiday, and all the strange creaks and groans I'd heard all night were just the house settling—whatever that means.

What I did *not* expect to see was the ghost of a recently murdered witch sitting on my favorite chaise lounge and staring at me with an irritated expression on her face.

"It's about time you showed up, Lexi Balefire. What on earth are you wearing?" Tansy Blankenship demanded.

I hadn't known Tansy in life, mind you—but I'd kissed her cold dead forehead a couple of weeks back, and that sort of forces the classification of *intimately acquainted*. I'd also been the one to light her funeral shroud on fire as our coven pushed her corpse out to sea. Just one of the perks of being the reigning Keeper of the Flame. Whoop-de-do.

"It's Halloween."

"It's Samhain, and you look ridiculous. Now, what exactly did you do with the other half of my soul?"

"What in Persephone's purse are you talking about?" I gaped at Tansy, still aghast that I was actually speaking to someone who should, by all rights, have moved on to the Summerlands to await her reincarnation as all other witches have done since the first of us rose to power.

Witch ghosts aren't particularly common, though I'd read about a few instances in one of the books lining the very walls surrounding us now.

"You can't be serious. You do remember that day in the mortuary, don't you?"

Oh, I remembered all right. The way Tansy's forehead had felt beneath my lips was burned into my memory. The smoky quartz pendant I'd worn around my neck had turned cold, and I'd stuffed it in a box in my bedroom and pushed the experience into the dark recesses of my mind. That's what you do when you're creeped out, right?

"Your soul is in my necklace?"

"Yes, as a matter of fact, it is. And I'd like it back

please unless you'd like one more person living in your house."

The head count had gone up to a solid nine—ten when my boyfriend slept over, and I cannot emphasize enough how much I didn't want to tag on number eleven.

"Well, obviously you can have your soul back." What an odd thing to say.

Easy enough. I'd give back Tansy's half soul, and she'd toddle off to the Summerlands leaving me plenty of time for my evening plans.

"It's in my room. Follow me." Except it wasn't. My number one faerie godmother is a huge neat freak. I've banned her from my closet, but she still manages to tidy up my room the second I turn my back. I'm twenty-five years old, for crying out loud.

How do I get myself into these situations? In the past six months, I'd had to save my boyfriend's soul from a cursed guitar, reunite a pair of soul mates determined to make me earn my designation of the best matchmaker on the east coast, and banish a Raythe to save the soul of one of my closest family members. And that's on top of shooting a flaming arrow at my grandmother.

Most people get up every morning and go to work

at a normal job; go home and watch mundane prime time television. They push papers or make French fries or plan fabulous parties. I get to deal with things like life and death, happiness and misery, eternal purgatory and...whatever the opposite of eternal purgatory might be.

Then again, most people don't get to live for centuries or have the ability to glamour their hair a different color every day of the week, or ride a unicorn through the backyard. I suppose I shouldn't complain. But that doesn't mean I won't.

With Tansy breathing over my shoulder—not exactly breathing, but you get the idea—I rifled through the workshop shelves.

"Somebody's a bit of a slob." I could have done without the acid comment. With Gran temporarily out of the picture, the workshop reverted to the way it looked when I'm the one in charge. Believe me; it's not an improvement. Half the supplies had vanished along with the elder relatives when they left for a few weeks of sun and sand.

"Thanks. Remind me again why I'm helping you."

"Because I'm haunting you and if you don't put me back together so I can go to the Summerlands, you'll have another new roommate. One who isn't happy to be here." Potion bottles rattled on the shelves and cauldrons echoed hollow booming sounds. "You help me, or you'll feel my wrath."

"Don't you threaten me, Tansy Blankenship. You're

screwing up my last day of peace before the house fills up with people again. I had plans for tonight, you know. I was going to watch Hocus Pocus and eat my weight in leftover Halloween candy, but no, you had to show up."

"I had to wait until the veil was thin enough to make contact. Get on with it, Lexi. I have things to do and places to be before the clock marks the witching hour."

"For Hecate's sake, you're dead. What's the urgency?"

"There's someone waiting for me on the other side."

Now that she mentioned it, I was getting the tickle in my belly that signaled a love match in the offing, and the Bow of Destiny had been chiming in my head all evening long. I thought the theme from The Addam's Family was its way of commemorating the holiday, but maybe it had to do with Tansy instead. What kind of creepy couple rates that as their romantic theme song?

"Why don't you help, then. I'm looking for a wooden box with a triquetra inlaid into the top. The workshop had a different configuration when Terra stashed it, so it could have migrated anywhere." It could have winked out along with the other items Gran seemed to think I wasn't advanced enough to access, too. "It's your soul, seems like you would have some idea where it scampered off to. Can't you sense its presence? I don't know why I'm the one stuck doing all the work while you rattle my shelves like a petulant child."

Tansy had the grace to look embarrassed.

"Reflex. It's a ghost thing. I'm sorry."

"It's okay. Tell me how you lost your soul mate."

Tansy drifted around the room, poking her ghostly finger into every box on the higher shelves while I took the low ones. A minute or two passed before she launched into the story of her lost love.

"Xander and I met at magic camp. You have, I assume, noticed that there aren't exactly a plethora of wizards to choose from."

She had me there. Growing up with faeries instead of witches kept me somewhat apart from the rest of my kind.

"Scarcity alone made him a catch. He could have been a toad, and every witchling in hearing distance would have thought him a prince, but he was so cute." Tansy practically swooned. "I've always been a something of a bookworm, and I never thought in a million years that he'd choose me out of all the other witches he could have dated. He was sweet, and he was kind. Xander had an affinity for animals; he'd spend hours in the woods conversing with the chipmunks, and once I saw him draw a white stag into a clearing and watched him pet it like a broken horse. When we turned seventeen, he gave me this."

Tansy held up her ghostly hand to display an exquisite blue moonstone set in an intricately-wrought silver band. Shiny hints of white, pink, and lavender swirled together to create a rainbow of color.

"It reminds me of the Milky Way; an entire galaxy in one stone."

"That was the point. He always said I held his world in the palm of my hand."

"What happened? How did he...you know...?"

"Faulty cauldron. Blew up in his face. It's one of the leading causes of death among novice witches. Did you know that? Statistics say at least two witches per century will die in a cauldron related accident." Tansy's voice fell into a mode that reminded me of my fourth-grade teacher.

"My familiar has lost several of his charges to exploding spells. I'm his ninth."

"His last life? That's a lot of pressure. Oh, I think I found it."

Sure enough. Terra *would* stash Tansy's soul in the darkest recesses of the dustiest shelf in the whole place.

Cold penetrated the lid of the box, and my fingers left melted oval shapes in the layer of ice crystals that had formed on the wooden surface. Inside, condensation caused the teardrop shaped smoky quartz to give off cold steam.

One time I made the mistake of touching my tongue to one of the poles holding up a metal swing set at school and ended up stuck there until someone got a teacher to help. I'd be willing to bet that pole had been a good deal warmer than the iced stone I needed to retrieve. Would I lose the skin off my fingertip if I touched the frigid surface?

Only one way to find out. Hesitantly, I reached for the stone nestled in blue velvet and felt the bone-numbing chill from an inch away. Using only my fingernails, I gingerly tugged on the chain until the pendant popped out of the box. Vanity to the rescue.

"There it is. Do whatever it is you need to do, and off you go."

Tansy's stare said many things at once, but they all amounted to the same sentiment. *How dumb are you?*

"What? Can't you just pull yourself together?" In my head, she was like mercury where you push the droplets together and they just sort of absorb into one mass. Don't play with mercury, by the way; it's poisonous if you're not a witch.

"Given I'm incorporeal, I guess not. You said you would help me."

Me and my big mouth.

It's not every day you need to mate the two pieces of someone's essence together, and I had no clue what to do.

Hundreds of books lined the workshop shelves and even if one of them contained some sort of ghost healing spell, my chances of finding it was roughly the same as finding a needle in a needle stack.

If my life played out anything like a TV show, there would be some foolproof method for finding what I needed. Maybe a book would fly off the shelf and open to the right spot like magic or I could tap on my book of shadows three times and watch the spell write itself in words of sparkling light. As it was, I was flying blind with no Dewey Decimal System to peruse conveniently, and for once no annoying familiar to point out my lack of studying habits.

An empty potion bottle launched off the shelf and whizzed past my ear—Tansy, reverting to her earlier level of impatience, protested my lack of haste.

"Give me a minute to think." A minute clicked by

and then another while I leafed through my grimoire in vain. "Any insights? You were a researcher, right? I'm not seeing anything useful in here." Putting broken ghosts back together probably wasn't a regular enough venture to rate a dedicated page in any of the books in the workshop. "Is there a trick to finding information?"

"Some people have the knack for it, some don't." To a normal human, a knack is some vague sense of intuitive ability. Witch knacks take the concept up a giant notch and often make themselves known at an age well before the Awakening, or onset of magic occurs.

A gifted toddler witch with a knack for—coincidentally—speaking to animals caused a newsworthy commotion at the park last year when every animal within his range flocked around the little fellow's stroller. The black bear incited the most panic when he made a beeline for the tyke, escaped his cage, and then rolled on his back in hopes of getting a good belly scratching. Some knacks are more useful than others.

"I'm pretty sure I have an anti-knack for research, so if you want to get this done, stop tossing doodads at me and help me find the right spell or ritual to put you back in one piece. You're nice enough..." Not being Fae, I had no trouble with the little white lie. "...But I'd like to get on with my evening."

"Give me a minute to think. I'm feeling positively half-witted tonight." As jokes went, it was a dry one and possibly unintended, so I suppressed a snort while Tansy zipped up to hover near the glass-domed ceiling. Nothing more useful presented itself, so I kept leafing through the book of magic and waited for her to come back with a verdict.

A few minutes later, she descended slowly. "I've lost it." Panic showed, or I think it was panic, on her face. Hard to tell what with all the shifting in the mist that made up her ethereal form. "I can't come up with a single reference to anything that would meld my two halves into one."

"What about..."

"I'm freaking out here." Restless, Tansy whirled around me like a dust devil running ahead of a storm.

"Settle down, you're making me dizzy, and I can't think straight when all I can worry about is not tossing my cookies." Okay, technically it would be my Twix bars, but the outcome would be the same.

I closed my eyes until the nausea passed and when I opened them again, Tansy had managed to rein herself in. The toe of her left shoe tapped soundlessly on the floor, and she gave me a steely stare over folded arms.

"Looks like we're in uncharted territory and I'm

going to have to write my own spell. Actually...” I suddenly realized that I had an edge in this situation. I dealt in souls every day; guided them to their other half, in fact. Why was I agonizing over something I can practically do in my sleep?

“All we really have to do is release this half of your soul from the quartz, and the best way I can think of to do that is to cleanse it. Technically, it’s dirty.”

“Thanks for that. If this doesn’t work, you just earned yourself some Poltergeist action.”

“Just shush, and let me work my magic.”

I flicked a finger and realized as a jar of salt and a bottle of distilled water flew across the room to settle gently on the table in front of me, that I was getting more used to using my magic every day. This was going to be a piece of cake.

“I know the salt water method is harsh, but it’s also the fastest way. Besides, I can guarantee I’m never wearing that necklace again, so it doesn’t really matter if the stone gets damaged.”

The recipe was simple. A scoop of salt in a wide-mouthed jar and fill the rest with water. Dip the stone, and clear its energy. Gingerly testing the chain to see if I needed a pair of tongs, I decided it seemed warm enough now to touch. Pinching the silver links between thumb and forefinger, I dunked the pendant, swirled it around a couple of times, then lifted it out of the salt water and waited to see what would happen.

Light speared out of the quartz in every direction while it swung frantically at the end of the thin silver chain. My godmothers would have been so proud of the disco lighting effect.

Under my feet, solid stone shivered hard enough I had to grab onto something to stay upright. Smoke poured off the quartz, engulfed, and blinded me. How was I supposed to use my soul-joining magic if I couldn't even see the two halves?

"Lexi, do something." Tansy shrieked, and I knew it was now or never.

Eyes tightly closed to keep from tearing up; I tuned into that place in my gut that knows a love match when I see one and found Tansy's former beau taking up the space where her two halves should be.

"Back off, Xander. She's no good to you in pieces. You'll get your turn."

The bow-toting daughter of Cupid who lurked inside me took notice of the situation. Her pink fire filling my head, I tuned into her energy and bolstered it with the power of witch magic.

Tansy squeaked again, and I opened my eyes in time

to see two outlines of her merge—light and mist—turn solid. Pink faded away along with my inner goddess, leaving behind a sense of rightness and accomplishment.

All that was left was to bid the young witch goodbye and wish her a happy trip to the Summerlands.

Or not.

CHAPTER

THREE

I stared at Tansy's ghostly form, which wasn't entirely ghostly anymore. I guess the veil between the living and the dead really was thinner on All Hallows' Eve because it looked as though I'd feel solid flesh if I reached out and touched her.

I didn't, just for the record.

In fact, I didn't say anything for at least fifteen seconds, which felt a lot longer in the lingering silence.

"Why aren't you in Summer? Are you still missing a piece?" You'd think she'd be able to tell.

"I'm whole. There has to be another reason." Tansy looked like she was about to cry if that was something a ghost could even do. Say it with me, people—there's only one other reason a recently dead person might want to stick around: unfinished business.

"Tansy, we've got less than five hours to fix this problem. What could possibly be holding you here?"

"I have no idea!" Tansy wailed. "I only had one enemy, and you and the rest of the coven made sure she paid for what she did to me. I'm a nice person. Was a nice person, I guess."

"There's got to be something, or you'd be riding on the golden chariot or whatever right now." I had no idea how witches got to the Summerlands, and if you want to know the truth, I had no desire to find out.

"Have you ever wronged anyone? Is there anything you need to make amends for?"

Tansy's eyes flicked back and forth while she racked her brain for the answer. You'd think if something bothered her enough to keep her from moving on to be with Xander, she'd know what it was.

"I have some overdue library books and a project for Calypso, but I can't see those being enough to keep me here. And a comforter I've been crocheting for the past three years."

I'd bet the number of people who reach the end of their lives with every project finished is so small it barely counts as a fraction.

"None of that sounds like the kind of thing that would keep a soul from moving on. The world would be full of ghosts if that were the case."

"There's one other thing, but it's so ridiculous. It can't possibly be the reason..."

"Spill. Before you're stuck here worrying about it for all eternity."

"Well, when I was a kid, my Great Aunt Bea had this teapot shaped like an elephant. It was candy apple red, the tail curled under to form a handle, and the water poured out through his trunk. When I'd come stay the night, Aunt Bea would enchant the teapot so the elephant would walk around the dining room table, and he'd trumpet the theme song to Sabrina the Teenage Witch."

"And?"

"Well, when my Aunt Bea passed away, the teapot was supposed to go to my mom's cousin, Hattie, but I wanted it so badly I stole it. I was twelve, and so ashamed of myself I wished it away to Shadow Hold."

Great, the same repository Clara had hidden the Bow of Destiny. The same place where Kin had almost been dropped into a bottomless abyss. And the same place where my mother had betrayed me and broken my heart.

"It's still there?"

"I tried to go back to get it after my Awakening, but someone had beefed up the wards, and I couldn't get past them. I never told Hattie, but every time I think about it I get sick to my stomach. Do you think that could be it?"

"I think it's our best shot at the moment."

"Do you think I'm a terrible person?"

"Tansy, you've got the tamest unfinished business I could have possibly imagined. We've all done things we're not proud of. I stole a lipstick from Ames once and felt so guilty about it I couldn't even wear it. Luckily for you, Hattie is still around for you to make amends. Ames went out of business a long time ago—probably because of people like me—so if it were my immortal soul hanging in the balance, I'd be screwed."

The thought seemed to cheer Tansy, at least a little bit.

"Thanks, Lexi. Really. I know this isn't how you wanted to spend your evening. But it's hopeless; we'll never be able to get into Shadow Hold, anyway."

"Don't throw in the towel just yet. Luckily for you, I happen to know a way in. It's not going to be a walk in the park, but we might just have a chance if we hurry."

. . .

When Kin left me the keys to his car, he never expected me to use them. Neither did I. Driving cars isn't my thing. Born for the city, I prefer to walk or putt along on a vintage Vespa with the wind in my hair.

Tansy floating along behind, I went upstairs to grab the keys. Every step brought another burst of anxiety. Multi-layered anxiety. What if I couldn't handle the 'vette? Or the night driving? And that was just half the problem. A night hike down a slippery hill and through the woods was fraught with opportunities to screw up.

Worry ricocheted through my mind like a pinball and Tansy finally had to yell at me to pull my focus back from the bowl with two sets of keys in it.

"Sorry." My hand hovered, and then I chose.

"We'll take Bluebell," I announced. If I had to go out into the woods at night, I'd at least drive the vehicle that made me feel safest behind the wheel.

"Who's Bluebell? I thought you were home alone tonight."

"Bluebell is the Vespa scooter I bought to replace the one Serena Snodgrass cracked up."

"Scooter? You want me to ride twenty miles on the

back of a scooter in the middle of the night? I don't think so."

What was the worst thing that could happen? We'd get in an accident that would kill her deader than she already was?

"Besides," Tansy continued, "it will take forever. What's the top speed on one of those things at night? It's faster if you skim."

"We'll drive." Skimming from one place to the next sounded like a great way to travel. In theory. If you knew how to do it and I didn't. Shame zipped my lips shut about the issue.

"We could fly. It's Samhain, what better night to be out on a broomstick?" Another gap in my knowledge base. Salem was right about me being a slacker.

"Can't you just, you know, ghost yourself there? Let me get there on my own if you don't like my choice of transportation."

Tansy's misty eyes shifted away. "There are rules."

"Rules about what?"

"Haunting someone."

"You're haunting me now?"

"What did you think this was? A friendly visit? I'm not Casper."

"I thought all the flash and bang was to get my

attention. I didn't know you were haunting me. And why me, anyway? What did I ever do to you?"

"Nothing. It's a haunting of convenience. You were there when my fragmented soul broke free, and so I tagged a ride home with you and then waited for you to figure out how to set me free. You're not the brightest match in the pack, you know. I tried everything I could think of to get your attention. Now, are you going to help me or not?"

"What if it's not? What then? Will you haunt me harder?"

"I've been watching you, you know. You're not as bad as everyone thought you were. I know you'll help me because you're a nice person."

"See, that's what I've been saying for years, but people still look at me funny."

"People don't know what to think about you. You don't see yourself very clearly, Lexi Balefire. And we witches stand out, whether we want to or not. You can't hide magic, but humans tend to ignore what's right in front of their faces. They explain away the things they don't want to see; a trick of the light, a coincidence, a daydream. You're not just witch, though, are you?"

Leave it to a ghost to figure out the one thing I hadn't told anyone outside my immediate family. It probably worked out better, since I had no desire to clue the entire coven in on my demigod status. At least not yet; not until I knew I could trust them.

"I'm a Daughter of Cupid. A Fate Weaver."

"I suspected as much. But I know how to keep my mouth shut. I wish Violet would have believed that. You could bet your butt I'd have stayed quiet if I knew how much it was going to cost me. But, there's no use crying over spilled blood, is there?"

"Tansy, I think that's the one thing it's okay to cry about." Drat, I was starting to like this witch.

"Look, I don't know how to skim from one place to another. Everyone in the community knows I didn't get my magic until it was almost too late. Since then, it's been seven levels of chaos, and there wasn't time for me to learn. Same goes for flying." I bared my soul because who was she going to tell?

"Skimming takes time to learn. If you're willing, I could um..." Tansy's ghostly face turned a delicate pink. "...do it for you." She ended on the kind of upswing that meant she was trying to get the point across without actually saying anything outright.

"How would you..." and then I got it. "You're saying you could possess me? No. Nope. No. No." The more I thought about it, the more I didn't like the idea.

"Then I'll teach you to fly."

Some thoughts come with an instant headache, this was one of them.

"I'm not sure that's such a good idea." For a hundred reasons at least.

"Don't be such a chicken. It's fun. Where's your broomstick?"

Saved.

"I don't think I have a flying broom. Aren't those a special type?"

"This isn't Harry Potter, Lexi. Any broomstick will work."

"What about a vacuum cleaner?" Hocus Pocus was still on my mind.

"Don't be ridiculous. Show me what you've got and we'll pick the best option."

Look, I'm thrilled to be a witch, it's a total hoot. But the idea of putting my entire weight on a stick between my legs sounded painful and stupid.

"See if there's one with a saddle of some sort." I pointed toward the half dozen rustic brooms poking out of an old umbrella stand. "Or maybe we can tie one of the sofa cushions around the handle."

Tansy trilled out a cute laugh. "You know you're

really funny. Like a witch comedian. Ever think of taking your act out on the road?"

Not if it meant flying there.

"This one will do." Tansy pointed to her choice: ash staff, birch twigs tied with flexible willow. A natural bend in the handle would make a lovely seat if there were such a thing. I was not looking forward to this at all.

"All you have to do is..." Tansy straddled the broom behind me and whispered a brief set of instructions in my ear.

"You're kidding. It can't be that easy."

"The hard part is steering."

"Don't forget flying in the dark." Ten other concerns crowded into my head.

"What kind of witch are you, anyway? There's a spell for seeing in the dark. Don't you read Witch Monthly? It's a shame not to keep up with current spells."

"Um. Sure. Slipped my mind. You don't happen to know how it goes, do you? I keep mixing that one up with the charm for warding off stubbed toes."

Tansy fed me the spell, which worked perfectly, but made me feel a little weird. With night looking like day,

I sucked in a breath, kicked off from the ground, and made my first ever broom flight.

I wobbled and bobbled for the first mile or so and then I got the hang of it. Tansy made side seat driver noises. The kind that make you want to kill the person because they never say what you did wrong, they just whistle in a breath between clenched teeth.

"You want to drive?" I yanked my hands off the handle and threw them up in the air. The broom would have nosedived if I hadn't clenched my knees hard enough to keep us moving forward.

"Sorry. It's nothing. I just think you're a little fast on the turns."

Just to show off, I poured on the speed, banked into a downward spiral, and touched down in the clearing at the end of the path leading to Shadow Hold.

"You ever been here before?" I asked.

"No, but I've heard stories."

"Believe me, none of them do this place justice. Stay behind me, touch nothing."

"It's not like I have a choice."

"If I tell you to run, you do it. No questions asked." Time, space, and the laws of physics meant nothing to Shadow Hold. For all I knew, Tansy would turn solid the minute we cleared the door. She needed to be prepared for anything to happen. Or nothing. So did I.

CHAPTER
FOUR

Shadow Hold occupies a charmed position in the center of two hundred acres of unclaimed forest. Charmed seems like a tame word when you consider the level of protections surrounding the repository of magical items deemed too dangerous to be housed anywhere else. Witches and wizards don't leave much to chance, especially when protecting people from certain magical mishap.

We touched down near the base of a familiar tree.

"This is it?" Tansy scoffed. "Doesn't look like much."

"No, this is just the perimeter. You can't fly directly into the Keep, so we have to get through the wards first." Now, who was the smarter witch? I pressed a series of knots in the order I remembered from my last trip to the hold. Given the choice of being forever haunted by Tansy or entering Shadow Hold at night, I was starting to lean toward welcoming Tansy to the family.

The path opened like magic. Naturally.

"Are we…"

"If you finish that sentence with the words *there yet*, I swear I'm done."

Tansy sighed and said no more until we topped the last rise and Shadow Hold lay before us.

Stone structures right out of a fairytale castle dotted the clearing and suggested the age of the hold predated America's official history by a few centuries. Good thing the perimeter wards shunted off curious normals because any historian worth his or her salt would lose their minds over a find like this.

"How did you manage to hide this damnable teapot here in the first place?" I asked Tansy. It hadn't been a walk in the park retrieving the Bow of Destiny from its hiding place, and I couldn't fathom how a novitiate witch might have gained access.

Tansy pierced me with an expression I didn't completely comprehend but hovered somewhere between irritation and disbelief. "I knew you didn't have much training, but I didn't realize just how little until right now."

"Thanks a lot," I responded dryly. "As if I haven't heard some variation of that comment about a hundred times by now."

Tansy at least had the decency to look chagrined. "I'm sorry, I didn't mean it like that. Shadow Hold is a kind of oubliette; there's only one way out, but you can throw whatever you want inside, metaphorically speaking."

"So you're saying anyone can toss an item in here; it's just the retrieval that will give you trouble?"

"Exactly."

I knew all about the second half of the equation since I'd already been there and done that. Didn't get the T-shirt, though. The first was something of a shock. Sylvana led me to believe only witches with the wisdom of the ages and a willingness to take on a guardianship role could access the hold.

"So there's no cadre of protectors who catalog artifacts and consign dangerous items here?"

"Maybe you're not as uneducated as I thought. Most witches consider the hold to be something of a magical trash heap while remaining unaware of any higher purpose. How did you figure all of this out?"

"Not my first time. Let's just leave it at that."

I like to keep my private history to myself, thanks.

"Any idea where to look?" I surveyed the dozen or so buildings and tried to remember if there were more today than the last time I was here. If the repository doubled as a magical dumping grounds, I hoped there was some method to the madness. Maybe a particular building for crockery disposal or other harmless items and only the really dangerous stuff ended up in the one-way horror with a bottomless pit in the center that I preferred not to visit again. "Because we'll be here until next Samhain if you don't."

"Picture the teapot the way I described it and cast a reveal charm. I'd do it myself, but I'm kind of dead here, so no magic."

"Red teapot in the shape of an elephant. Got it." In my mind, the elephant took on a playful quality, like something out of a children's book. Keeping that image, I whispered "Revelare," and waited.

"I don't think it worked."

"You pictured an elephant, right. Not a hippo or a rhino."

"For Hecate's sake, Tansy. I know what an elephant looks like. I was raised *by* faeries, not *in* the Faelands. I'm familiar with the species."

"There is more than one type of elephant." Tansy went into lecture mode. "Asian, African—forest and bush—Indian..."

I cut her off right there. "It's a teapot, and it's red, I

hardly think minute variations between species is what I'm missing here."

"The variations are hardly minute, ear shape, tusk length, size, and color are all factors."

"It's a teapot, not an actual elephant. Can we focus on the problem at hand?"

Agreeable to a fault, Tansy tried three times to give me a better mental image and failed miserably.

"This isn't working."

"There's one more thing I can try," and before I had a chance to ask what, Tansy possessed me. Only for a second, only long enough to show me the teapot, and still I wanted to crawl out of my own skin.

"You could have asked." Creepy, cold needles raised goosebumps on top of goosebumps and gave me the worst case of the heebies I'd ever suffered.

"Revelare." Ice wouldn't have melted on my tongue my tone was so cold.

"Sorry, I didn't know what else to do. And you would have said no, anyway."

"Good thing it worked," my nod indicated the shaft of light arrowing out of the thatched roof on the building to my immediate left. "Let's get this over with." The sooner, the better.

Not caring if she followed, I stalked to the door and tested the lock.

"What is your business?" A ghoulish face with glowing red eyes popped out of the wooden panel.

"Dude, seriously. Your breath." Gag me.

"Oh, sorry." The face turned to the side. "Can I help you?"

"This one lost a teapot in here a long time ago, is it okay if we go in and take a look?"

"Are you willing to sign a waiver indemnifying management in case of death or dismemberment?"

"Whatever it takes, we're in a bit of a rush." Formalities observed, I led Tansy into the darkness "Be prepared for anything, touch nothing," I warned. My last trip included some stringent testing of my will and fortitude.

"As if I could."

Tansy's night vision spell saved me having to conjure up enough witchlight to get my bearings. The interior of the circular building expanded to triple the size it looked from the outside. A staircase spiraled in both directions, disappeared into mist above and darkness below. Millions of items spilled from shelves to pile on the floor at each level.

"Revelare?" I didn't mean to end the charm on a tentative question, but that's how it came out. The idea of finding the teapot in a room of infinite possibility seemed too daunting a task even for magic to handle.

Magic must have thought so, too, because nothing good came of the spell. Nothing at all.

"Try something else," Tansy urged.

"You try something. This is your unfinished business, not mine."

"You know I can't cast."

While we bickered, I moved deeper into the space and Tansy followed me. "Didn't you brag about having a knack earlier? Use it to figure out how, or even if, this stuff is organized."

Drawn to take a closer look, I left Tansy to her own devices and made my way up the stairs to the next level where something flickered and glowed. Hey, I like shiny stuff.

Tansy's muttering comments echoed up from the floor below. "Color, date, type. Nothing makes sense. Usage, maybe? No. That's not it."

Thousands of broken broomsticks, cracked cauldron, and potion jars tumbled amid a vast array of items. This truly was a dumping ground. Nothing looked especially dangerous, but the glow I followed never seemed to get any closer. I went up another level, and then another leaving Tansy behind, forgotten.

I don't know how many stairs I climbed, but based on the way my legs felt the next morning, it must have been a lot. Finally, tucked into a niche in the wall, rested the object of my obsession, and I got a closer look at the fancy, cut crystal potion jar.

Sealed with a blood red stopper and a heavy layer of spelled wax, the jar held a creature of exquisite, bird-like beauty. Blue shading toward green, each tiny feather begged the touch of a finger to determine if she would be as soft as she looked. Hummingbird wings spun the air inside the jar, holding her aloft as she hovered and watched me with naked hunger. If I gave her freedom, she seemed to say, she would grant my heart's desire in return.

Enthralled by her beautiful need, I ran a finger over the glass, clenched fingers around the stopper, and started to pull.

Tansy's presence invaded my mind a second time as she possessed my body, removed my hand from the bottle, and screamed in my head.

"You idiot. What were you thinking?"

Icy fingers of ghostly creepiness sliding through my

body were enough to pull my mind back to the present. The insult just ticked me off.

"What? What is wrong? I was only helping this..." I glanced at the demonic spawn flapping greasy batwings against the side of the bottle and showing rows of wickedly sharp teeth. "...Oh. Never mind. That was a close call."

"While you were up here attempting to wreak havoc on the world, I figured out the storage system. Let's get the teapot and get out of here before you do major damage."

"I didn't mean to; I didn't know. She looked so beautiful and helpless."

"It's okay; I'm sorry I called you an idiot. I think being dead blocks glamour and if I'd been in your position, I might have let her out myself."

Her kindness banished some of my shame, but not all. To protect the next unsuspecting person who passed through the oubliette, I stuffed a musty old cloak into the niche to block the jar from view. "Eat dust, you old bat."

"Come on, we're running out of time, and the teapot is a few floors down. It's fascinating, really. They're using threat levels as a means of classification."

"You mean the more dangerous the item, the higher

it's stored?" Made as much sense as anything does in the witchy world.

Ten minutes later, teapot in hand and happy the travel ban only worked in one direction, we lifted off from the valley of Shadow Hold.

CHAPTER

FIVE

We scrambled back out the entrance of the repository at exactly 11:15, which left us only forty-five minutes until the witching hour when, according to Tansy, her ticket to the Summerlands would expire.

Tansy's cousin (once removed, or however the heck that works, I can never remember) Hattie lived clear across town, and it was a good thing we had flown because with all of the holiday debauchery going on downtown, we'd never have made it in time.

"Won't Hattie be at the Samhain ritual with the rest of the coven?" I asked, mounting the broomstick.

"No, not this year. They canceled the whole thing in light of what happened with Violet Bloodgood. From what I've overheard, Calypso decided to stay home and tend to Serena. Personally, I think she was peeved that several of the members refused to attend without your grandmother and Aunt Mag present. She's saving face, but at least Serena's getting some mothering out of it. I know you two don't get along, but she's not so bad, Serena."

"It's water under the bridge," I grumbled as we floated over the bright lights of Port Harbor.

Hattie Blankenship's house looked exactly the way a witch's house is supposed to look. A Victorian-era lattice design adorned the double gabled roof, giving the impression of two eyes with arched brows. Ivy climbed the walls, and an overgrown hedge kept passersby from becoming too nosy.

"Go on. We have some time before your deadline." I prodded Tansy up the brick walkway. She took a deep breath before raising a hand to knock on the door.

"I'm going to need some help here," Tansy called to me over one shoulder.

"Oh, right." I joined her, wishing I wasn't about to get dragged into someone else's emotional moment and clicked the brass knocker loudly.

Hattie opened the door and, looking back and forth between her dead niece and me, did the not-so-witchy thing and turned a pale shade of green.

"Letitia, you'd better come here. RIGHT NOW." Her voice was shrill as she pulled me inside and motioned for Tansy to follow.

Now, it might sound like the chance of a lifetime to

get to say goodbye to your loved one who has passed on, but in reality, even for witches, it's unnerving at best.

Letitia, still clad in funeral black, emerged from the recesses of the house and mimicked Hattie's reaction at Tansy's presence.

"But you're...you...Tansy. How?" Letty's hands folded over her breastbone, probably to keep her heart from breaking out of her chest. Even in the dim porch light, I could see the pulse point at the base of her throat throbbing.

"We don't have a lot of time," keeping my tone gentle, I eased my way inside. The interior of the house matched the exterior about as well as an elephant matches a mouse. I'd expected period styling, but not this particular period. The only thing missing from the quintessential fifties decor was Donna Reed buzzing around the kitchen in a perfectly tied apron.

"Tansy's here to return this and say goodbye." I handed the teapot to Hattie and headed for the door. As far as I could tell, my job here was done. Tansy could say her piece, apologize to Hattie, and move on to the Summerlands without me.

If you thought that was a reasonable assumption, you'd be as wrong as I was.

The door banged shut, the lock clicked by itself, and I didn't even bother testing my strength against it in a struggle sure to distract during Tansy's precious final moments with her family.

"I'm not even sorry I stole your teapot if it meant a chance to say goodbye." Tansy addressed Hattie, but her eyes remained fixed on her mother's tear-stained face. "I don't have a lot of time, Lexi needs to..."

"Take all the time you need." What were movies and candy compared to the important things in life? Or death, to be more accurate. "I'll just be over here." Trying to fade into the woodwork, or failing that, the cushions of the tweed sofa.

She turned to her mother, "I'm afraid I've monopolized Miss Balefire shamelessly."

On the plus side, the distraction of our short conversation allowed Letitia a moment to pull herself together. Hattie gave her cousin a one-armed hug, then joined me while mother and daughter spoke.

"It's okay, Mama. I know you're dying to say it."

Say what? I felt like the worst kind of voyeur watching what should have been a private moment.

Letitia's *I told you so* burst into the air and was followed by a nearly incoherent rant along the same lines.

"...listened to me, you would still be here." Breathing hard and sobbing out her pain, Letitia berated Tansy for leaving her and broke my heart in the process.

"I'm sorry. It's little enough to say, but it's true. I should have trusted your intuition, and I didn't listen." The quiet admission took the wind out of Letty's sails, and she nearly deflated again when the anger that had held her up was gone. Tansy moved in to lay a spectral hand on her mother's cheek, and the love in her eyes undid me.

"My girl, my baby. I..." As if the words stuck in her throat, Letitia fell silent.

I heard Hattie sniffle and wished I had adopted Aunt Mag's old-ladylike habit of stuffing a tissue in her sleeve. I could have used one right about then.

"Don't cry. Please, don't cry. I'm not gone away, just gone on ahead, and I'll be waiting for you. Don't close yourself off, and don't grieve too long, okay? Miss me a little, but live your life and maybe say yes to a date with that nice man who keeps calling."

Letitia's eyes widened in surprise and Tansy teased, "You thought I didn't know? He makes you smile, and I want you to be happy."

"You were my life, my heart. My girl."

Tansy leaned close, whispered something into her mother's ear. Whatever she said seemed to come as a surprise judging by the look on Letty's face before fresh tears gathered in her eyes.

I had to turn away then; it was too hard to watch mother and daughter share such a touching farewell.

"It's time. Goodbye, Hattie. I'll miss you both. I love you." Tansy faded away and unable to face a second more of Letitia's pain, I excused myself.

Outside, there was one more surprise. Tansy waited. I checked my watch. Twenty minutes to midnight.

"We have just time enough to move on to our next stop."

"Our next what?" The witch was holding out on me.

"It will be fast, I promise." Tansy tossed a rueful smile my way. "We have one more mission tonight, Lexi."

"So this wasn't your unfinished business? When did you figure that out? And when were you going to tell me?" When you try to frown and glare at the same time, your face gets confused."

"Well, I might have fibbed about that part of it, but I really did need to return that teapot, and there were things I needed to say to my mother. Please don't be mad at me."

How could I? The poor thing wanted a few precious minutes with her loved ones. I'm not a total jerk, and after spending time with her, I would miss Tansy when she finally did leave. If she ever bothered to go at all. I was beginning to wonder about her plans.

"Where to?"

"I need to visit the place where I...where it happened."

"Oh. Are you sure it won't be too traumatic?"

"No, but I have to go. Please, won't you take me?"

I was starting to suspect she'd transition to the Summerlands at midnight with or without my help and this had all been a ruse to get me to cart her all over town and back.

"Climb aboard. Who needs movies and candy when there's a real life ghost story playing out?" I owed her for the secret to broom flying anyway.

This particular flight lasted only a couple of minutes.

"Right here. This is the place."

Whatever I expected to see, it wasn't a normal stretch of street far enough out of town to be slightly lonely, and a lot less well-lit than my own. Nothing sinister marked the scene of Tansy's demise. We'd barely touched down when she leaped off the broom to go rooting around in the bushes.

"It has to be here. I just know it."

"What? Tell me, and I'll help"

Tansy held out her hand and showed me the ring on her nearly solid, but still ghostly finger. "Xander's ring fell off my hand during the fight. I need to find it before I go. It's important." Frantic, she turned back to the search.

I couldn't see how. Based on all the evidence she'd shown me this evening, even if she found it, Tansy couldn't touch the ring, so what was all the fuss about?

"Um. Revelare." This time I had a perfect image in my head, no possession needed. Tansy pounced on the spot at the heart of where the thin beam of light began.

"It's here. Oh, Lexi. You did it, and just in time, too. I'm so happy. Now listen close."

My watch showed thirty seconds to midnight. Whatever Tansy had to say, she'd better get to it and fast.

"The ring belongs to you now. It has strong magic, so use it wisely."

What was it with magic rings? "What does it do?"

"I'm sorry, it's too late. Goodbye, Lexi. And thank

you." As Tansy's voice faded out, so did the night vision spell—not that I needed it at the moment because there was plenty of light coming from a spot behind her body.

With a final wave, Tansy turned toward the white stallion and the man riding him, the love who had come to take her home. Such joy infused his face that I found myself both smiling and crying as Xander welcomed his love to the Summerlands.

"Blessed be Tansy. Blessed be."

I tucked the ring in my pocket and flew home.

SHOT TO SPELL

A FATE WEAVER NOVELLA

CHAPTER
ONE

I shoved the covers off and stumbled into the shower with only one eye open and not even all the way at that. A swath of rainbow-hazed, heart-shaped bubbles drifted out of my shampoo bottle, and I knew this was only the beginning of the holiday I'd been dreading for weeks.

It could be that all faerie godmothers are obsessed with hearts and flowers on February 14th, or maybe it's only mine. As much as I love them, this was one year when I could do with a little less enthusiasm.

No, I'm not a bitter old hag who has never known true love—quite the opposite, actually. I am a matchmaker, so love is my stock in trade. In my world, every day is Valentine's day. Except with less pressure to perform a romantic miracle. I mean, what am I, Cupid himself?

Well, I'm not.

I am his daughter, though, and I carry his bow and arrows, so I guess that makes me Cupid-adjacent.

Reaching into my closet, I grabbed an entire outfit in basic black. No pink. No red. Just unrelenting black to indicate my feelings this year. Why should I buy into the arbitrariness way some card company decided sales could be better in February and forced half the world into believing one day was more romantic than the rest?

My dad isn't the cute little cherub portrayed on candy boxes either, in case you were wondering.

The scents of chocolate and roses filled the kitchen where the dance of the faerie godmothers was almost too much to take. I'm blessed with four of them, and they're the proprietors, or should I say, perpetrators, of Enchanting Events, a party planning company. Hence the chocolate and roses.

"What's for breakfast?" Please let it be pancakes, I thought. Pancakes are my go-to cure for grouchiness.

"Pancakes. Chocolate chip." The news brightened my spirits until Terra qualified, "Heart-shaped." Oh, bother.

"Never mind. I'll grab something on the way to work."

"Don't be foolish, you love pancakes."

"No. Just no. Make them any other shape, and I'm all over it, but not hearts. Not today. I can't take it."

Terra's face changes when she gets annoyed. Her eyes flare like twin flames, her cheekbones fine down to razor sharpness, and you'd think after a lifetime of dealing with the fallout from faerie temper tantrums, I'd learn to avoid being the cause of one.

Probably never happen.

"A good breakfast is the best defense against a bad day."

"You should embroider that on a pillow, but I'll take my chances." The flip comment earned me a narrow-eyed look, but Terra let it go without trying to teach me a lesson. Being Fae, her responses tend toward the literal, and being the elemental faerie of earth, when you get a dirty look from Terra, it frequently comes with actual dirt.

I didn't have time to take a second shower, so I was thankful she'd let this one go.

"You should really listen to your godmothers, Lexi." My familiar, Salem, lectured me through a mouthful of pancake.

"You've got a little something brown on your nose, there, Salem." I hissed, chuckling to myself as I watched him lick the space between his thumb and forefinger and wipe at his nose in a fitting, feline gesture.

The scent of freshly brewed heaven called my name

as I passed Java Java Java on the way to the office, and I couldn't resist so I went inside to orchestrated chaos.

"Grande Caramel Macchiato. Wait, better make it a venti, double caff." I gave my order to the barista wearing the Valentine version of the ugly Christmas sweater and moved toward the end of the counter where I hoped coffee would soon appear.

A flourish of music echoed through my head. Seeing as its preferred method of communication is music—often loud music—I've wondered if my dad used harp strings when he fitted the Bow of Destiny. Like today when my brain rang with the sound of a thousand violins.

"Okay, I get it. Lay off." It wasn't hard to figure out the bow's intended target—the puffy coat-wearing redhead with the fabulous boots. The glittering, pink heart only I could see floated over her head and marked her as my next shooting victim.

If I hurried, there would be time to lance her heart with Cupid's arrow before the perky little blond behind the counter finished decorating my coffee with caramel swirls.

To answer your next question: no, I did not yank out a four-foot long bow made of living gold and take aim at her right in the middle of a crowded coffee shop. I'm not a psychopath. That honor is reserved for the Goddess who lives inside me. The part of me that comes from my father's gene pool. She's the one who does the dirty work and, thankfully, no one but me can see her.

A graceful predator, my weapon-toting half slid out, took aim, and fired a golden arrow with perfect precision. The other half of my heritage kicked in just before the arrow hit and pinpointed the redhead for what she was. Another witch.

Wait, did I forget to mention how, on my mother's side, I'm descended from a powerful line of witches? My name is Lexi Balefire, and I wear many hats—only one of them is pointed with a gleaming silver buckle above the brim. No one bothered to explain this to me until recently, but when mommies and daddies—if they are Cupid and a witch anyway—love each other very much, they make Fate Weaver babies like me.

Normally, I wouldn't have been called upon to carry my father's bow, but there were complications, family drama, and to make a long story short, I became the reigning Cupid.

A sudden tinkling noise issued from the puffy coat as my arrow passed through it on the way to the witch's heart. I remember thinking something along the lines of *how odd* in the seconds before all hell broke loose. Except in very specific circumstances, my arrows are more metaphysical than physical in nature. In other words, they pass through items, and even hearts, without leaving a mark. For it to break the vial of potion the witch carried in an inside pocket was not business as usual.

Nor was the panic on the redheaded witch's face when she saw the spreading stain on her coat. Coffee forgotten, I crossed the space between us and asked in a low tone, "What kind of potion was it?"

Her answer came with raised eyebrows and a grim twist of the lips. "Love."

Of course, because what else would it be on Valentine's day in a packed coffeehouse? Like ripples around a stone dropped in a calm puddle, the essence of love potion spread throughout the room leaving no one untouched. Well, except for me and..."What's your name?"

"Dahlia Breedlove. From over in Hannigan Cove."

"Lexi Balefire. What was in that potion?"

"The usual, brandy, cinnamon, rose, and of course my own special addition of—" Dahlia clapped a hand over her mouth. "Let's just say it's a family secret."

"Oh for Hecate's sake. Does it look like there's time

for playing coy?" By then, the potion had infiltrated the atmosphere in the coffeehouse and charged the whole place with some of love's baser emotions. A sickly sweet scent permeated the air, and suddenly a squat, balding man behind the counter started to look a lot like a Magic Mike cast member. "Fine, you deal with this then." I barreled past Dahlia and flung open the door before whatever pheromone-enhanced concoction she'd brewed could further alter my perceptions.

Outside, the chill washed the fuzzies out of my head, and I realized I needed to stick around and help clean up the mess. It was at least partly my fault. But I wasn't going back inside without putting up some kind of decontamination barrier to keep all the love cooties away.

Hours later, having missed all my appointments for the day, in the seconds before the oblivion of sleep swallowed me whole, I vowed to spend every February 14th in a cocoon. For the rest of my life.

CHAPTER

TWO

I shoved the covers off and stumbled into the shower with only one eye open and not even all the way, at that. A swath of rainbow-hazed, heart-shaped bubbles drifted out of my shampoo bottle, and I didn't think anything of it until the scents of chocolate and roses assailed my nose at the top of the stairs.

"What's for breakfast?" Please don't let it be pancakes, I thought for the first time ever.

"Pancakes. Chocolate chip. Heart-shaped."

Everything looked the same as it had the day before. Terra wore the same Kiss the Cook apron over the same red dress while the other three godmothers added roses to the top of a three-layer torte.

"Er...I'll pass."

"Don't be foolish, you love pancakes."

"No time. Clients." And a severe case of deja vu.

"A good breakfast is the best defense against a bad day."

"You really should listen to your godmothers, Lexi." Salem mumbled.

"Yeah, I think I heard that somewhere before." I ran out of there like my butt was on fire.

I spent the entire walk into the city failing to convince myself everything I was seeing was not the same that day as the day before. The jogger in a blue jacket slipped on the ice, but caught his balance before falling, and then walked away like he meant to do that—again. The toy poodle dancing on the end of a hot-pink, rhinestone encrusted, patent leather leash did her business on the sidewalk—again.

Morbid curiosity drew my feet toward the coffee shop, the promise of clearing my mind with a hit of caffeine pulling me inside. Same ugly sweater, same madding crowd, and right in the middle of it stood Dahlia Breedlove with the glittering pink heart floating above her head.

Like everyone, I have those moments of insanity where I repeatedly run the vacuum over the piece of lint that won't come up. I've even picked up the offending fluff, then put it back on the floor to try again. What I wasn't going to do was shoot Dahlia with the bow this time. Nope. Not going to happen. A repeat of that disaster wasn't on the menu. For once, I ignored the jangling melody playing in my head, took my coffee and walked away.

"Real mature," I murmured when the bow blew me the stringed instrument version of a raspberry.

According to my schedule, I had a first meeting to engineer in a few minutes. Matchmaking clients only end up in my office as a last resort after trying and failing to find love on their own. Making the process less clinical is a priority; after all, who wants to tell their grandchildren the story of how they finally gave up and went to see a professional dating adviser?

Today's fortunate victim was one Rusty Boneck. Slightly shy, with a good sense of humor once you got him talking. Gorgeous eyes behind dark-rimmed glasses, and a runner's build.

His intended, a sweet-natured woman named Sherry worked at the North Street dog shelter. Yes, I did stalk her a little. It's what I do. Some matches are pivotal enough to rate attention from the Bow of Destiny with a song and shining symbol. Others, the less intense ones, give me a little jingle in the gut that pulls me toward someone's perfect match. I call it my L.P.S. (Love Positioning System). When my stalking took me into her workplace, the lovely Sherry tried her best to talk me into adopting the most adorable little mutt. Salem, my cat familiar, would not have been amused.

A fifteen-minute ride in a cab together ought to give her enough time to bring Rusty out of his shell. And it would make a sweet meeting story, too.

I arrived at the corner of Eighth and Crombie just in time to toss a speed-up spell on the 9:40 crosstown bus and when poor Sherry hit the curb she saw nothing but taillights as her ride turned the corner on Ninth.

Cue Rusty right on schedule, bless his little heart. I hit send on a text telling him I'd been delayed and he should meet me at...what a coincidence, Sherry's work address. He absorbed the text just as the cab I'd ordered came into view.

His arm went up, and a short distance away, so did Sherry's.

For a minute there, it looked like a flawless plan playing out just the way I intended.

All I needed was to get close enough to orchestrate the taxi stopping right between them and let nature run its course. Worst case, I might have to toss on a glamour and suggest they share the ride. Keeping the lower half of my face tucked into my knitted scarf and the upper half covered by my hat, I slid into the space between Sherry and the bus stop vestibule.

My gaze flickered between the cab and the man and the woman. The driver was coming in just a touch too fast and would overshoot the mark giving Sherry the chance to jump in before she and Rusty could converge. My slow-down spell—just a hint of it, should do the trick and I'd give them a first meeting to remember.

I swear I didn't choose the wrong wording. For Hecate's sake, I'd just done the speed-up spell, so I knew the difference. But speed-up the cab did. And not only a little, either. The driver shot to the curb through six inches of a sloppy slush puddle which promptly spun out from behind the tire and rained down in an ice-cold, dirty wave that slammed into Sherry before soaking me to the skin.

Gasping, Sherry pushed a muddy strand of once-auburn hair out of her eyes and looked for the reason.

"You. That was my cab you tried to steal, and now look at me." She lit into a gaping-mouthed Rusty.

"I didn't...I'm sorry."

"Say something charming. You can do this." I muttered and kept my face averted while a glut of icy water shivered down my neck. "Come on, Rusty." People meet under worse circumstances every day, and this could be salvaged. They could still have a cute meeting story unless he blew it by saying something stupid.

Or worse. Smirking.

"Do you think this is funny? What a jerk." Sherry cast a look over her shoulder that would have slagged bedrock into lava and headed for home and dry clothes leaving Rusty behind.

I was half tempted not to bother shooting him another text saying I'd have to postpone our appointment, but I gave him the benefit of the doubt. Shivering and annoyed, I sneaked into the nearest hidden spot and took myself home using magic. There are some perks to being a witch even if I was having the worst day ever.

Again.

CHAPTER
THREE

I shoved the covers off and stumbled into the shower with only one eye open and not even all the way, at that. A swath of rainbow-hazed, heart-shaped bubbles drifted out of my shampoo bottle, and I didn't even bother going downstairs to see if heart-shaped pancakes were on the menu.

Only a fool fails to learn from the past, so I crawled back into bed, yanked the blankets over my head and contemplated who had reason to curse me into repeating this day. I'm a good person—kind to strangers, wouldn't kick a puppy, and I spread love in the world; what could be nicer than that?

Salem scampered into the room and transformed into his human guise before my very eyes, "Don't you have some work to do today? Get your lazy bones out of bed and come down for some chocolate chip pancakes. They're extra special today—heart-shaped, in honor of Valentine's Day."

"Go away, Salem. I'm not hungry."

"You sure? A good breakfast is the best defense against a bad day."

"Get out of my room, or I'm bringing home a puppy." I glared at him until he whirred back into his kitty form and scampered out the door.

In the midst of reviving my pity party, I rolled over and went back to sleep.

The next morning, I shoved the covers off and stumbled into the shower with only one eye open and not even all the way, at that. A swath of rainbow-hazed, heart-shaped bubbles drifted out of my shampoo bottle which, in a fine fit of pique, I winged into the trash.

Ten minutes later, I held up a hand to stop Terra telling me what was for breakfast, and left the house before she could finish warning me about the perils of ignoring the first meal of the day.

Right on cue, slip-on-the-ice guy slipped on the ice. The yapping poodle dropped her load just in time to ruin a nice pair of pumps.

Walking past Java Java Java, I glared in the window. The coffeemaker in my office would have to do. At the end of the block, I remembered my impending appointment with Rusty, texted to cancel, and congratulated myself on getting this far without incident.

Pink hearts popped up like demented jacks-in-the-box during the eight-block walk to the office. Under normal circumstances, I'd whip out my bow like a wild-west gunslinger, pop pop pop, and blow the smoke from the tip of my arrow's heart-shaped barb with a wink and a smile.

Instead, I decided to go back to my roots—to the nature of my job before the Gods insisted I level up. Flix, my business partner at FootSwept Matchmaking, was already in the salon out back, and before I scuttled through the connecting door, I confirmed that every one of the gaggle of women anxiously watching the clock was his client and not my own.

"Hey, Lexi, what's shakin'?" Flix asked, in far too jovial a mood for my tastes. His usually platinum blond hair had been faerie glamoured to a rose gold sheen and slicked back into a 50's-era pompadour complete with a single curl threatening to bob into his line of sight at any second. A pair of gleaming gold shears whisked through the strands of the client seated before him at a speed Edward Scissorhands would envy.

The recently-wed Mrs. VanDerVeen peered help-lessly at me when he spun the chair away from the mirror, her expression darkening as Flix continued his whirlwind cut and style. Not until he'd whipped off her drape and ceremoniously revealed her reflection did the concern recede from Mrs. VanDerVeen's eyes.

"Voila!" Flix pronounced with a flourish. Perfectly tousled ringlets framed her symmetrical face, and paired with the right little black dress and smoky eyeliner, she was sure to give her new husband one of the best nights of his life.

"What's with the line out the door?" I asked as Flix ushered in the next harried-looking woman.

"I'm overbooked." He shot over his shoulder.

"Overbooked? How?"

"Well, I have more appointments than I have time to finish." He explained with a signature eye roll. "I made the mistake of letting Salem answer the phone one day last week, and I think this is his way of getting back at me for some long-forgotten transgression."

"Yeah, that sounds about right. Let me help." Finally, a task I could accomplish without messing anything up. Or so I thought.

With a lighter heart than I'd had in days—relatively speaking—I checked the client list and called Mona Katz into the salon with a spring in my step. Not only was Mona a former client, but she'd become a good friend, besides. Plus, she'd been bragging for a week about how her new assistant was such a gem they were ahead of schedule. Mona is an artist and cake is her medium of choice.

"Getting ready for a date with Mark?" I asked, already knowing the answer.

"Sure am. Lexi, I think Mark is going to propose tonight!" Mona's pathetic attempt at a whisper reached Flix's sensitive Fae ears, and when we rounded the corner arm-in-arm, he began humming the wedding march at the top of his lungs.

"I won't say congratulations—you know it's bad luck if he hasn't actually gotten down on one knee yet —but Mark's a smart man, so I'm sure they'll be forth-coming." Flix shot Mona a wink and finished rinsing shampoo from a head of jet black hair.

Mona and I chatted during her shampoo and condi-tion, contemplating outfit choices and deciding that a trim and some burgundy lowlights for her long blond layers would strike the perfect balance between sexy and "future wife."

Now, before you ask, the answer is no. I am not a trained stylist, but I am a trained witch with a little Goddess added in for good measure and am more than capable of whipping up a glamour spell more potent than permanent hair dye.

It's a common misconception that witches need

wands to work magic. Magic comes from the elements: the five major, overarching elements of earth, air, fire, water, and spirit; and more specifically from every element on earth whether identified by modern science or not. In one quick flick of my finger, I beckoned what was necessary to erect a sight barrier, and projected an image of me physically cutting and styling Mona's hair.

Meanwhile, behind the veil, I closed my eyes, raised Flix's spare pair of shears, conjured a vision of my desired final outcome and reopened them expecting to see Mona looking fabulous and ready for the most important night of her life thus far.

Instead, she sported a purple mohawk with neon green tips.

"Oh. My." I gasped, praying the sight barrier also effectively blocked the expletive from reaching Mona's ears, and looked to Flix with panic written all over my face.

He did a double take while I desperately tried to undo the damage. Mona's hair cycled through several other bizarre styles including a 1970's pageboy a la Florence Henderson, the Rachel layered shag in shades of blue and yellow, and finally a look that resembled what I would have accomplished had I actually made the attempt without a drop of magic. A big chunk of hair was missing, right in the middle of the back of her head. No matter how hard I tried, no amount of glamour—witchy or Fae—would fix my mistake.

"Um, Mona, I hate to tell you this but...we have a problem."

"That's not something I really want to hear, Lexi. What did you do?" I'd never heard anything quite so sharp escape my friend's lips, but her words were like razors.

"Well, I...accidentally...um..." I looked at Flix with desperation in my eyes.

"You're getting a bob." Flix pronounced, followed by a slew of calming words full of phrases that reassured Mona she'd be on the cutting edge of fashion, and that Mark would be so blown away by her new 'do he'd want to ask her to marry him twice.

While Flix took care of Mona, I retreated between the racks of clothes we keep on hand for matchmaking clients and searched for what I hoped would serve as a peace offering to my friend. Finally, I located a fire engine red, silk Versace cocktail dress and a matching pair of stiletto pumps in Mona's size.

Mollified, she walked away looking gorgeous—no thanks to me. When we were alone again, Flix fixed me with a withering glare.

"Good Goddess, Lexi. What is up with you today? Did you wake up on the wrong side of the bed or something?"

"No, just the wrong side of the space-time continuum."

"Maybe you ought to give up the coffee, start your day with a good breakfast. You know, it's the—"

"Best defense against a bad day." I finished for him. "I'm starting to believe that's the god's honest truth."

CHAPTER
FIVE

I shoved the covers off and stumbled into the shower with only one eye open and not even all the way, at that. A swath of rainbow-hazed, heart-shaped bubbles drifted out of my shampoo bottle, and I knew that this was only the beginning.

Scratching lather into my scalp, I breathed in lavender-scented steam and let it soothe away the top layer of stress. If my life was going to take on the quality of a holiday TV movie, I'd better embrace the concept, learn my lesson and move on.

As far as I could tell, the whole debacle began with my bad mood however many days ago...or today since I was still in time warp hell. And why wouldn't I be cranky this year? Over the span of a mere nine months, I'd gained my magic (which came with a side of unanticipated extras), and both my mother and grandmother had come back from the dead. Talk about having your world rocked, and as the cherry on the top, I'd found my true love and then lost him again. No wonder I found this particular Valentine's day bittersweet.

Still, that was no reason to inflict my pain upon the world at large. Given a choice between being bitter and using my experiences to become more compassionate, I'd choose the latter. The decision lightened my mood.

Giving in to the inevitable, I pulled on a soft red sweater over a pair of black slacks and paid extra attention to my makeup. Might as well embrace the day if it was the only one I was ever going to have again.

At this point, I looked forward to an office full of Valentine's Day hopefuls—as long as I could make it to work without setting off any major catastrophes.

"Do I smell chocolate chip pancakes? I'm starving." Terra got a kiss on the cheek as I passed her on my way toward the coffeemaker. "Those look delicious." My plate had magically filled while I added cream and sugar to my cup. "You remembered caramel syrup is my favorite. Thank you."

"Can't send you off to work hungry, now can we? After all, a good breakfast is the best defense against a bad day."

I pasted a smile on my face and hoped like spell she was right before jetting out the door.

Another bright smile caught Clumsy Jogger Guy's

eye just in time to hit him with a confidence boost that turned his fumble into an impressive hurdle that scared the toy poodle onto the snow-covered median and saved his owner's shoes from certain doom.

A belly full of chocolate, caffeine, and a newfound sense of hope put a spring in my step as I approached the door to Java Java Java just in time to see Dahlia Breedlove's puffy coat exiting the establishment. The Bow of Destiny's orchestral arrangement evolved into a Stevie Nicks tune I couldn't help humming along with.

When a handsome man sporting the same heart symbol as Dahlia rounded the block and appeared in my peripheral vision, I whipped an arrow from the invisible quiver strapped to my back and let my inner Goddess out of her cage. Two quick shots hit their marks, and the couple's symbols began shimmering to the same beat. I didn't even have to watch what happened next to know that soon, the pair would share True Love's Kiss and become mated for life, but I couldn't resist observing the besotted look that crossed Dahlia's face as she made eye contact with her soul mate for the first time.

Satisfied and burgeoned by unexpected success, I made it to Rusty and Sherry's corner a little early. Like clockwork, heart recognized heart in the touch of a hand on the door of a cab. A tiny tear formed in the corner of my eye when they zoomed off into the sunset. Okay, it wasn't sunset or even sunrise, but you get the drift.

By the time I arrived at FootSwept, I was breathless and riding the high that always accompanies the successful mating of souls. The front office was empty save for two clients who, as luck would have it, were actually meant for one another, and had already begun the delicate dance of flirtation without any additional help from me.

Leaving them to it, I poked my head into the salon and, for a moment, wondered if I'd been transported to the Land of Oz. Flix and all four of my faerie godmothers were churning out Valentine's Day date hairstyles with more panache than the girls from the Wash & Brush Up Company.

Evian, with her command over the element of water, held court at the shampoo station with the help of Terra, whose anti-dirt charm was more effective than a professional scalp treatment. "Head on over to Flix, honey, and he'll fix you right up."

Magic hung heavy in the air, and the customers never noticed a thing out of place.

The assembly line culminated in a joint effort by

airy faerie Vaeta and fire wielder Soleil that rivaled Flix's own legendary blowouts. I'd hardly noticed the current client was Mona until she'd bounded out of the barber's chair and nearly knocked me over with an excited hug.

"Lexi, you'll never believe it! I think Mark's going to—"

"Ask you to marry him tonight?" I finished without considering the fact that Mona didn't remember our last salon encounter. Good job, Lexi. How does that foot in your mouth taste?

Mona raised an eyebrow but apparently chalked it up to my unparalleled matchmaking skills, "Yes, and I need something really special to wear. Do you think I..."

"The red Versace will be perfect."

WHEN SPELL FREEZES OVER

A MAG & CLARA BALEFIRE NOVELLA

CHAPTER

ONE

"There's a dead elf in the snowbank out front." Hagatha Crow announced to no one in particular. It was the third time in a week she'd slipped away and pointed her tennis ball-footed walker toward her former residence.

Deep in a discussion, let's just call it what it was—a feud—over the name and makeup of their new business, sisters Clara and Mag Balefire ignored both Hagatha and her outrageous statement.

"Soaps and lotions. That's what we agreed on." Clara tapped the sturdy toe of one pointed shoe on the floor with impatience.

A large sign leaned up against the front counter of their new storefront. Even with opening day weeks away, the finer details, like what wares to sell and what to call their new venture, might doom their fledgling business before it ever had a chance.

"I like antiques. Old stuff sells."

"So do toiletries." Clara flicked her wand toward the

ecru-colored surface of the blank sign, and the words Lotions and Potions appeared there by magic.

"When, in our hundreds of years of history, have I ever declared a love for soap?" Mag pulled out her own wand with a flair and the sign shifted to read: Knicks and Knacks. "I didn't mean that the way it sounded and you know it," she clarified when her sister snorted.

"Probably at about the same time I developed a fondness for dusty old notions." Another flick and the sign changed again. This went on for some time until old Hagatha decided she'd had enough.

"Stubborn fools."

A witch of advanced years—so many of them it was speculated they could be counted in millenniums rather than centuries—Hagatha required no tools to work her magic. She merely looked at the sign, and the letters arranged themselves to read: Lotions and Notions.

"You," Hagatha pointed a bony finger at Mag, "can stock the place with antiques, use some of the furniture as a showcase, for her," the gnarled digit turned toward Clara, "soaps and unguents. Best of both worlds, everybody wins. Now stop acting like children and do something about that dead elf before it rots and stinks up the town."

Shown the possibilities of combining their two passions, the sister witches dropped the competition and began brainstorming. They ignored any mention of the elf; old Haggie must be imagining things.

"She's right. We could take out all this sterile shelving, bring in some elegance. I'm seeing amber and blue glass bottles with our logo on them, all lined up on polished wood with strategic lighting to make them shine."

"Well, I hate that name, though." Mag balanced Clara's enthusiasm with a touch of her typical grumpiness. "Lotions and Notions. Might as well call it Gunk and Junk." A twitch of the eyebrow showed the grouchy only went surface deep. "It could work, though. With the right pieces."

"Snowbank. Elf. Dead." Booming with enhanced magical strength, Hagatha finally got the attention of both sisters and stomped off toward the door as quickly as the walker, and her spindly legs would allow.

"We'd better go see what the old bat is going on about before she freaks out the entire neighborhood again." Clara couldn't decide if Hagatha was in the process of losing her mind—which was the coven's prevailing theory and the whole reason she and Mag had taken over the place. Or, if being older than dirt,

Hagatha no longer gave a tin whistle about censoring anything she said or did.

Neither situation would be good for the local witch population, and both meant more headaches for her and for Mag given they'd unofficially taken charge of the coven while letting Hagatha think she still held the reins. Witches had no trouble hiding in plain sight in a city the size of Port Harbor, but here in the boonies, as Mag liked to call the area, magic was harder to conceal.

Harder still when the coven leader had a wild hair up her butt about the need for keeping things under wraps. As far as Hagatha was concerned, witches should be free to lead their lives out in the open, and the rest of humanity could just suck it up. Once determined to follow this course of logic, the old witch made it her mission to use magic as often and as openly as possible.

Toward the middle of November, Hagatha embarked on a one-woman rampage that nearly got the whole town plastered all over the news and triggered a series of increasingly frantic phone calls to the Balefire sisters. Skyclad, grinning maniacally, and holding her broom aloft like a baton, Hagatha had led her version of a Thanksgiving day parade straight through the center of town. A crazy, naked woman could be explained away fairly easily. Twenty enchanted turkeys singing "I Put A Spell on You" could not.

It took a joint effort from six covens worth of witches to craft an effective enough memory charm to wash away the spectacle. Clara and Mag had been offered control of the coven on the spot, and while they would rather not have had to deal with Hagatha, the idea of starting over someplace new appealed to both.

And so, that is how it came to be that Mag and Clara now found themselves staring down at the very dead, red and green clad elf lying in the snowbank in front of their new home.

"See. Dead elf. What'd I tell you? Toss it in the trash before someone sees it. I thought you two cared about appearances, and if anyone else discovers a rotting elf carcass on your lawn, you'll have a bigger mess to clean up than a dead body." Heart of gold, that Hagatha.

The poor creature lay sprawled over the back side of the freshly plowed snow which was the only reason passersby had not yet noticed the tragic figure.

"Yes, well." Clara searched for the appropriate response, while Mag, who had more experience with magical creatures, hunkered down to check for a pulse.

Looking up at her sister, Mag frowned and shook her head.

"It's not dead," came the solemn pronouncement. "Close, but not entirely."

"We'd better take it inside before it freezes to death out here." Raised in a traditional witch household, and one of the most powerful witches in a handful of centuries, Clara Balefire had not the first clue how to tend to a sick Christmas elf. Still, her tender heart would only be satisfied once she had made an effort to save the poor thing.

"Cold won't hurt it. Snow is one of the main ingredients when it comes to making Christmas elves."

"Making?" Clara slid gentle hands under fragile shoulders while Mag laid hold of the ankles above the curled tips of bell-laden shoes. A cheery jingle sounded when the sisters heaved the elf's body off the ground.

"It's gonna die and stink up the place. Dead elves smell like candy canes." Hagatha predicted darkly and then cackled out a laugh as she shuffled back inside and let the door slam behind her.

"Thanks for all your help, Haggie," Mag muttered.

"Do you think her parents knew what she'd turn into when they named her?" Clara used a touch of power to turn the knob, and nudged the door open with her butt. "Can you make it up the stairs? Or should we just put him on the floor behind the counter? Away from prying eyes."

Only eight years separated Clara and Mag by the calendar, but to look at them, you'd swear it was ten times that number.

"I can carry it up there by myself and don't you think I can't." Mag blew a fluff of white hair out of snapping dark eyes. "Just because I look like I could have dated Methuselah, doesn't mean I'm decrepit or incapable of doing things." A couple of centuries spent tracking rogue magic had taken its toll on Margaret Balefire's appearance. A choice she'd made knowing the consequences, and for that, Clara respected her sister even if she liked to tease from time to time.

"Pyewacket, Jinx!" Clara called, and two cats immediately jetted into the room with a flurry of fur, took a good look at the elf cradled between their masters, and raced back out of the room with their tails puffed out to three times their normal girth.

Every witch has a feline familiar—a companion with a plethora of knowledge whose life is inextricably linked to his or her charge. Each familiar is blessed with nine lives and nine corresponding witches. Pyewacket belonged to Clara, and Jinx to Mag.

"What's that about? I guess they're not going to be any help to us in this situation. I'll make sure to hide all the smoked salmon before breakfast tomorrow."

"Kitty kibble it is. Can't wait for that argument. If they ever decide to switch back to human form, of course. We don't need them anyway; we got this. Grab its feet."

"Can you tell if it's a boy or a girl?" Calling the elf an *it* all this time seemed like a form of disrespect to Clara.

"Not by its feet, if that's what you're asking. And I'm not exactly in a position to see anything else at the moment. Besides, I wasn't planning to check and see if it had any jingle bells if you know what I mean."

Clara suppressed a smile as she made an effort to take more of the elf's weight. Despite her sister's assurances that the aged look went only skin-deep, Clara had seen Mag leaning heavily on her cane at times and knew there was more physical damage than her sister wanted to admit. "I wasn't asking you to, and you know it. Let's hurry; one of us needs to go back down and see to Hagatha. I don't like leaving her in the shop by herself."

"She's a keg of dynamite waiting on a fuse," Mag agreed. "Someone ought to tie a bell around her neck, so they know when she's escaping."

"Oh, I'm pretty sure that niece of hers is the one holding the door open. Wouldn't you do the same if you had to deal with her all day?"

"You do have a point."

Hagatha's voice tinkled from below, "You know I can hear you, right? And the elf is a boy, obviously." Clara and Mag shared an eye roll and a wry grin as they made their way up the stairs.

"Saw that too," Hagatha's assurance rose up behind them.

CHAPTER

TWO

"Here, in *Hargraven's Guide to Mythical Creatures*, it says: *Christmas elves, a creation of the wizard known as Santa Claus, require a constant supply of Christmas spirit to survive, and rarely venture far from the North Pole, where their source of energy is most potent.*" Mag paced the upstairs spare bedroom with the helpful volume two inches from her face, deftly sidestepping piles of boxes still waiting to be unpacked without taking her eyes off the page.

Clara's brow furrowed, "I wonder what he was doing so far away from home. Poor little thing." The tenderest of hearts, she couldn't bear to see anyone or anything in pain. "Let's see what we can do to make this room more festive. Maybe that will enhance the elf's Christmas spirit."

"It can't hurt," Mag agreed, tucking *Hargraven's* into a nightstand drawer and pulling out her wand.

Clara did the same, and with a flick of her wrist an old phonograph wheeled across the floor, the merry notes of Christmas music emitting from its weathered brass horn, "That ought to get us started."

Humming along, and allowing holiday cheer to fuel their magic, the sister witches summoned every Christmas decoration—and anything red, green, silver, or gold that could qualify as such—into the bedroom.

No fewer than four ornament-laden trees filled the room with a riot of color.

"I really like the pink and white lights, but can you kill the blinkers? The flashing gives me a headache," Clara grumbled.

"This one needs more tinsel." Mag gestured, and an absolute avalanche of the stuff fell over the blue spruce clad in red and green plaid ornaments. "Oops, too much." Half the tinsel faded, and she surveyed the results with a tilted head. "That's better." In fact, Clara liked it so much, she made a complicated gesture, and the tree zoomed into the living room where it took up space in the center of the bay window overlooking the street below.

"It looks like a craft store sale two days after New Years in here," she looked around doubtfully, "Shouldn't we at least try to make it less gaudy?"

"I don't think the aesthetic makes much difference, and besides, this is probably what it looks like at the

North Pole. Santa's not exactly known for keeping things low-key. You think it's a coincidence that before the Halloween costumes have gone 50% off, you can already buy tinsel and twinkle lights? The gaudier, the better, I'd wager. Now, let's sing."

"Sing?"

"Yes, to activate the magic. Sing, and think about Christmas Eve when we were kids."

Clara closed her eyes and, with the lilting lyrics to "Silent Night" rolling off her tongue, joined in Mag's recollection. Scents of cinnamon, sugar, and butter filled the air as Clara recalled pulling sticky globs of yeasty dough from the tower of homemade monkey bread their mother, Tempest, constructed each year. One portion always ended up tucked into a cache near the chimney, a treat for the reindeer who always managed to avoid detection no matter how hard Clara tried to catch a glimpse.

For Mag, the magic of Yuletide rested in reciting traditional spells and reading the omens for the coming year. Hanging holly and mistletoe over each threshold and above the fireplace for protection made her feel safe. And, of course, there was the Christmas pudding. Making a wish while she stirred, always clockwise in the direction of the sun.

With each happy memory, magic bubbled and churned and grew into a visible haze of sparkling motes that coalesced into a stream of festive, multicolored glitter. It snaked through the air, and finally made a beeline for the prone elf, shooting into his nostrils with a resounding boom.

The little guy stirred, some of the color returning to his cheeks. His eyelids fluttered once and then stilled again, but a tiny smile remained on his thin lips.

"Well, it sort of worked. We just need more juice." Mag pronounced.

"Look, there," Clara pointed toward the ceiling where a faint glimmer sparkled against the age-darkened paint, "It's another trail of Christmas spirit, and it's headed downstairs. Let's see where it leads us."

"Good catch, little sister." Mag's tone was entirely complimentary, but it still made Clara feel like a child. But there were more important things than a temper tantrum, and giving in to the temptation to throw one wouldn't go far in proving herself otherwise.

On her way by, Clara tossed a blanket over the elf. Sick people, in her experience, tended to do better when cuddled up and comfy.

Reclaimed by her niece during the decorating extravaganza, Hagatha was nowhere to be seen, and for that small mercy, Clara felt thankful. The woman reminded her of a geriatric pit bull. Taking the lead, she trailed the magic essence out the door and down the street with Mag following close behind.

Harmony homeowners apparently viewed decorating for Christmas as a prime competitive sport. That was the only explanation Mag could find for the absolute glee and abandon with which the town had embraced the many manifestations of the twinkle light. They glittered, and flickered, and chased roof, door, and window outlines. They dripped from eaves, blanketed shrubs in glimmering webs, and that was just the start of the madness.

Each house, Clara was happy to note, in the row leading to the single-street shopping district known as downtown, was different from the next. No cookie cutter neighborhood, this. And the houses had some breathing space between them.

"Oh Mag, look at that one." Rigged up on a metal structure, the tableau of Santa's sleigh taking off without him inspired a chuckle. The manikin of the jolly old elf carried an expression of consternation as he reached toward the runaway sled. Gifts spilled from his bag; his hat set askew on his head. "It's so very clever."

"You're already planning something. I can see the

wheels turning, but let's not get distracted. The trail is stronger now, do you see it?"

It wouldn't have taken a crystal ball to predict which house the spirit trail would lead to, the sheer magnitude of decorations gave it away. If there were fewer than a thousand strings of lights winding up tree trunks, and along the eaves of the gingerbread trim, Mag would lick a stinkbug.

Plastic candy canes and lollipops festively fenced the property on three sides. Every window sported a wreath, the door was wrapped up like a gift, and the porch held an entire scene made from brightly-painted wooden cutouts. A herd of lighted, wire-framed reindeer frolicked behind a fence wrapped in glittering gold garland on the left half of the lawn. An entire workshop's worth of plastic and wooden elves danced across the right. There was more than the eye could take in all at one go.

All of that showed an unparalleled dedication to the art of decorating for the season, but it was the thick blanket of Christmas spirit that had called Mag and Clara to this place.

"Holy Hecate, would you look at that?"

"The name on the mailbox says *Granger*, and there's the coven symbol etched into the front door frame. This is Gertrude Granger's house." Clara pulled the details from her steel trap of a memory, having read through the list of coven members prior to accepting the position in Harmony.

"Anything sketchy on her record?" Mag asked.

"Nope, she's older than us—I believe she'll celebrate her quincentennial this year—and not a black mark to speak of. Coven secretary, and once upon a time she was second in command to old Haggie. But, Gertrude stepped down for unrecorded personal reasons about a century ago. Seems an odd thing to do. Maybe there's something to it. She missed the whole Thanksgiving parade debacle, too."

"You know how easy it is to step over to the dark side. It's not out of the question. She had to get all this Christmas spirit from somewhere, and I don't believe in coincidences. Put on your high priestess hat and let's find out what's been going on here."

Clara straightened her shoulders and approached the front walkway, snow crunching beneath her feet. Christmas spirit virtually poured out of the chimney like wood smoke, and when Mag jabbed the doorbell, they could hear Jingle Bells chiming from inside.

The woman who opened the door looked nothing like what either Mag or Clara expected; five hundred years isn't all that long for a witch to live, and Gertrude Granger looked more like a toned-down fifty-something cougar than a grandmotherly old spinster. With less than thirty-six hours to go before midnight on Christmas Eve, she was dressed in a modest yet hip-hugging version of Mrs. Claus' outfit, complete with a cotton-trimmed velvet skirt and matching Santa hat.

"Merry Christmas!" Gertrude boomed as she welcomed the sisters into her cinnamon and balsam-scented foyer. "You're the newest members of our coven, aren't you? Balefire witches?" Her aqua blue eyes sparkled with excitement.

Both women nodded in assent. "I'm Mag, and this is my sister, Clara."

"Nice to finally meet you, would you like a cup of cocoa?" A twirl of her finger conjured three mugs and a doily-lined plate of peppermint-speckled fudge. "Candy cane white chocolate, have a taste."

It might have been all the Christmas spirit zinging around the place, but suddenly white chocolate candy cane fudge and hot cocoa sounded a lot like the nectar of the gods, and it was a full fifteen minutes before the poor, unconscious elf crossed Clara's mind again.

"Thank you for your hospitality, Gertrude, but we didn't come here to eat you out of house and home."

Clara began, keeping her tone friendly and non-threatening.

Mag interjected before the poor woman had a chance to answer, brisk and to the point, "Just where did you happen to come across such a high volume of Christmas spirit?"

Clara sighed; this was Mag's way, and probably always would be. A big bulldozer, Mag would raze an entire field trying to pick a single flower.

Gertrude looked between the two as though questioning their sanity and replied, "What do you mean, come across? The holidays are my favorite time of year, and I work quite diligently to spread cheer. In fact, I'd call it a full-time job, considering the state of the world we live in today. Do you know how many children don't believe in Santa Claus nowadays?"

"Well, yes, it's quite sad, really, but..." Clara's response got lost in Gertrude's excitement.

"Just last night, in fact, I managed to make believers out of half a dozen kids, thanks to a gentleman friend of mine, a simple glamour, and a chimney engorgement charm. You should have seen the looks on their faces. I never had any children of my own, you know, but I volunteer at the community center and the children's hospital over in Charleston."

"You sound like a regular good Samaritan," Clara said pointedly, shooting dagger eyes at her sister.

"Yes, she does," Mag agreed, but she returned Clara's glare with a raised eyebrow and exaggerated side-eye motion which pulled Clara's attention to the wall of bookshelves and to the fireplace mantel where a veritable army of Elf On a Shelf dolls cavorted.

Bearing an uncanny resemblance to the elf currently riding their spare bed, the little dolls were arranged into a series of amusing vignettes.

"Do you mind?" Clara crossed the room for a closer look. "However did you come up with all these ideas?"

In one scene, three elves clustered around a half-finished snowman made from marshmallows. Another featured an elf stranded on a beach after a sleigh crash, complete with palm trees and HELP spelled out in tiny sticks and stones. A closer look at the upturned face revealed an expression of fear that was a little too realistic.

"So creative, and such attention to detail. How do you make them look so life-like?" Doing her level best to maintain a curious tone, Clara pried. "It's uncanny."

Could Gertrude be capturing real elves, harvesting their Christmas spirit, and turning them into dolls? The idea was enough to make Clara shiver and reconsider her love of the porcelain-faced beauties. Never mind that the elf on their sofa seemed more likely to melt into the ether than to shrink to doll stature, the notion of him being trapped and forced into one of Gertrude's theatrical displays lodged like a splinter.

"Mag, you have to come look at this, it's the cutest thing." Anyone who knew Clara well would recognize the false cheer in her tone as a warning of some type. Mag certainly did and joined her sister while Gertrude practically beamed.

"Look at those little faces. How did you find dolls with such varied expressions? I'd love to get in touch with the manufacturer, we could carry these in our shop next Christmas," Mag followed Clara's lead and practically gushed, but her hand slid into the pocket where she kept her wand and a few handy defensive potions. Mag might be out of the dark hunting game these days, but some habits never die.

Face reddening under a layer of artfully applied makeup, Gertrude mumbled something about not revealing her source and Mag elbowed Clara in the ribs.

"Ow!" Clara whispered and returned the favor before putting on her most intimidating scowl. "We know you're hiding something, now out with it. There's an elf's life hanging in the balance."

"A real live one?" Gertrude's face registered a series of emotions. Shock followed by shame, and then an avid curiosity.

"Of course it's a live elf. How could it's life be hanging in the balance if it wasn't alive?" Mag's patience for foolish questions could best be measured in fractions of an inch. Her willingness to point out the obvious, though, was at least a mile long.

"Can I meet him? I've always wanted to meet a real, live Christmas elf." When Gertie clapped her hands like a little girl, Mag lost her last ounce of control.

"Have you or have you not been stealing Christmas spirit from elves and then using their husks in your little theater of pain here?"

Every drop of blood drained from Gertrude's face, taking it from a dull flush to a pale mask.

"What is wrong with you? How could you even suggest a thing like that? I love Christmas and elves. I would never...I could never. Oh, Margaret Balefire, you're a horrible person for thinking anything of the sort. You should be ashamed of yourself."

Mag recognized truth when she saw it. She'd been playing the game long enough to identify a dead end when the wall stared her in the face.

"Maybe there's a way Gertrude can help us out with

our elf problem." Gently, Clara turned her attention to the older witch, who now sported a guarded expression. "But first, where did you get these?"

"I make them." Eager now, Gertrude spilled the truth out of ruby-painted lips. "I've spent years perfecting the spell for generating Christmas spirit, and I still can't make live elves, only these," a ring-laden hand gestured toward the shelves. "Poppets. It's the best I can do. I've concluded that Santa adds a secret ingredient besides those listed in Hargraven's because I think my Christmas spirit is every bit as strong as his. I use only the purest driven snow and the finest hot chocolate, too."

"I wouldn't be surprised," Mag stated matter-of-factly, "He's gone to quite a lot of trouble ensuring nobody knows too many details about what happens up there, and I doubt he would have given away one of his proprietary methods so easily."

Clara noted the crestfallen look on Gertrude's face and an idea began to take shape in her mind, "You know what, Gertrude, maybe there's a way we can all get what we want. We've got a languishing elf at home, and you've got enough excess Christmas spirit to save him."

"You mean you'd let me see him, talk to him, maybe

even ask him a few questions about his, er, constitution?"

"In exchange for enough magic to revive him, absolutely." Clara agreed.

"Let us go back home and see if it works first," Mag cautioned, for once the more conscientious sister, "No sense making promises we can't keep."

Positively giddy, Gertrude left the room for a moment, returning with a gilded potion bottle that sparkled with inner light.

"This is my best stuff. It's from the most potent batch I've ever made. I keep a few bottles handy just in case. You call me, and I'll drop everything to come and meet that elf."

THREE

A cold northerly wind had sucked one side of a set of old lace curtains through the kitchen window. Clara saw the flutter of white as soon as she and Mag turned the corner.

"I thought this was a safe, quiet town," Mag grumbled. "Looks like we've been robbed."

"I don't think so." Hagatha's walker stood next to the front steps. "But it is a home invasion of sorts."

"Don't know why she bothered to move out if she's going to be here every ding-dong day." Ding-dong had not been the phrase Margaret meant to say, Clara could tell by the look on her sister's face. Hagatha had left a few handy charms on the old place, and an anti-cussing spell was among the more annoying ones.

That old Haggie had chosen to substitute her own phrases for those spoken within the confines of the property made Mag's verbal gaffes even more hilarious to her sister. In a fine fit of pique, Mag stomped up the steps, tried the door, and found it still locked.

"I don't care if I have to wallow through snow up to my badonkadonk," Clara hooted until she nearly cried at the idea of Hagatha even knowing that word, much less preferring it over whatever Mag had been trying to say. Eyes slitted and sparkling with barely contained ire, Mag continued, "I'm doing a cleansing ritual to rid the place of her influence if it takes fifty pounds of salt and a garden full of sage."

"Okay." The giggles still coming, Clara agreed. "I'll help." Keeping the peace might be less amusing, but was probably the best course of action.

The rooms at the top of the stairs felt even colder than the air outside because Hagatha had turned off the heat and conjured an industrial-sized fan to blow on the elf.

"What were you thinking putting a blanket over a Christmas elf? Don't you know anything about the species? They're made of snow and magic. He was practically transparent by the time I got here."

Clara looked and felt chagrined, unused to being in the proximity of a witch with so much more knowledge and experience at her disposal. "Oops. I didn't even think..."

"No matter, he looks much better now. And we've managed to get our hands on some concentrated

Christmas spirit, so let's see if we can revive him enough to get him back to the North Pole." Mag thundered across the bedroom and perched herself on the edge of the bed. "Down the hatch," She placed one thumb against the little guy's chin and not-so-gently pulled his bottom lip open far enough to deposit the swirling mist directly into his mouth.

With a cough and sputter, the elf stirred. His eyes fluttered open, and his gaze darted back and forth for a moment before he hit panic mode, "Where am I? Who are you? What happened?"

"We'll be the ones asking the questions. What were you doing down here anyway? I thought Christmas elves stayed in the North Pole." Mag got straight to the point, making no effort to comfort the creature and causing Clara to sigh and push her sister aside with a harder-than-necessary shove.

"I'm Clara, this is my sister Mag, and this is Hagatha," Clara gestured to the senior witch who, for once completely silent, watched with amusement. "We're not going to hurt you; we're trying to help." She added with a gentle smile.

"Yes, yes, I can see that. I'm sorry. I came here because someone has been stealing elve's Christmas spirit. I need to find whoever it is and return the culprit to the North Pole before...before it's too late. It's almost Christmas Eve, and there's important work to do."

"Tell us exactly what happened. We're witches; maybe we can help."

The elf held up a tiny hand in the gesture that means stop. While Clara and Mag waited, he took a moment to compose himself, and then rolled his eyes up and to the right as though accessing his memory bank.

"Clara and Margaret Balefire; daughters of Tempest, mother and aunt to Sylvana, grandmother and great-aunt to Alexis. Correct? Yes, I believe you are trustworthy. I permit you to help me."

Mag and Clara exchanged a look of annoyance, "Is there some sort of hobknocking briefing about the Balefire clan circling around? Why does everyone and their grandmother seem to know who we are?" Mag grumbled and ignored the fact that her words had once again been censored.

"Well, if it makes you more comfortable, my name is Evergreen Goldensparkles, and I happen to be Santa's right-hand man. It's my job to compile the naughty and nice lists every year, and neither of you has been on the naughty list since you were children." He shot a pointed look at Mag.

"It's nice to meet you, Evergreen. Now, please, explain what we can do to help."

"Didn't you just hear him, or do you have cotton balls stuffed between your ears?" Hagatha piped up from the corner, "Obviously, someone hijacked his connection to the Christmas spirit, and if he doesn't get it back he'll fade into nothingness and cease to be."

"Is that all of it?" Clara's eyes burned daggers at Hagatha, who she vehemently hoped would disappear instead. The brief conversation seemed to have taken its toll on Evergreen Goldensparkles, because Clara had to give him a second dose to keep him from fading away on the spot.

"Yes, precisely," Evergreen sighed, "I followed the trail from the North Pole all the way here, but then I was attacked out of nowhere. Must have...tipped off..."

As he talked, Evergreen turned paler by the second. Either Gertrude's spirit-brewing skills were not as potent as she thought, or she had been right about Santa leaving an ingredient out of the recipe when he'd give it to Hargraven.

"Tipped who off? Tell me who did this so we can help," Clara implored.

He gasped, "Elf. Not like me. Name is Ja...." With that, he lapsed back into an unconscious state leaving the sister witches staring at each other in consternation. Mag dumped another dose into Evergreen, but it wasn't enough to rouse him.

"Haggie, you know more than we do about elves, can you keep an eye on him while we try to track down whoever did this? They couldn't have gone far. Keep the Christmas spirit going and try to keep him alive while we're gone," Gertrude's bottle passed into Hagatha's hands, "it won't be a very fun holiday if we kill an elf before the eggnog's been served." Mag sprang into problem-solving mode and began to delegate. Haggie agreed with a bit more enthusiasm than necessary, leaving Clara wondering what condition the place might be upon their return.

"Yes, of course, he needs to conserve his strength. One thing, before you go." Hagatha held out a hand, and a thermometer appeared in her palm. Into Evergreen's mouth it went, and after a few seconds, she pulled it out, wiped off any moisture on the back of her pants, and handed the fragile glass to Clara.

"It'll measure how much Christmas spirit he has left. Get back here before it's all gone. Now, there is one place someone looking for the holy grail of Christmas spirit might go in this town—The Harmony Holiday

Hullabaloo, which takes place tonight at the community center." Hagatha offered.

"Organized by Gertrude Granger, right? She mentioned it was the culmination of her fourteen days of Christmas celebration. Gone a little overboard, hasn't she? Most people do twelve."

"Gertrude Granger doesn't have a lower setting. But she's got a heart of gold, and she's one of the most generous women in town. Mind your manners, little lady." Clara's ears turned candy apple red, and Mag couldn't suppress a grin wondering if they were about to pour steam.

"I'm a couple of hundred years old, I'm hardly a "little lady," she grumbled once Hagatha was out of earshot.

"I heard that, and you're still practically an infant compared to me."

"That woman has ears like a hawk," Clara muttered.

"It's eyes, but I get your point," Mag agreed, "She's going to be a handful."

"Understatement of the year. Now, we need to come up with a plan, and I think I know exactly where to start." Mag followed her sister downstairs to the shop, where Clara searched behind a counter for some paper and a pen. "We're calling in reinforcements. This is Santa's mess; he can come clean it up. I want to be back in Port Harbor by the time Lexi and the faeries start their midnight snack on Christmas eve."

"What are you planning on writing? *Dear Santa, if you want to see your elf alive again...?*" Mag affected a deep, Italian accented voice in a perfect impression of Don Corleone.

"You really don't want any gifts this year, do you?" Clara chided, but the reproach held no weight considering the gigantic smile on her face. She might be a big, fat, pain in the badonkadonk, but Clara wouldn't change her sister for all the magic in the world.

CHAPTER
FOUR

Held at the town hall, the Harmony Holiday Hullabaloo had Gertrude Granger written all over it. In glitter and canned snow. Armed with the enchanted thermometer and very little information about who they were looking for, the Balefire sisters braved the winter wonderland-themed party. The decorating committee had outdone themselves in shades of blue and silver and white.

"Hagatha would have had a field day with this," Mag commented when she got a look around the room. Coven members made up a tiny portion of the attendees with the rest of the throng being townsfolk who weren't supposed to know they lived among the magically inclined. "Good job convincing her we were too stupid to look after the elf without her help."

"Speaking of Evergreen, we have to figure this out fast. Look!" Evergreen's spirit meter showed the barest hint of glimmer at the lower end of the glass. "We're almost out of time." Whispering loudly, Clara poked Mag with her elbow.

"Think I don't know that?" Mag scanned the crowded room with an eagle-sharp gaze. Hopped up on the excess of Christmas spirit thanks to Gertrude's ministrations, several likely suspects sported sparkling auras more dense than the rest of the spirit coloring the air. She dragged Clara toward the front end of the great hall and through the door where a set of steps led to a curtained stage.

Dust lifted off thick blue velvet when Mag twitched it aside to peer out over the crowd from the elevated platform that gave a better vantage point.

"I count six possibles," she said.

"Same here. We can rule out Gertrude and her familiar, don't you think? That leaves four."

"And I think those two kids are probably okay, too. They're too young to be that diabolical."

Together, Mag and Clara focused their attention on the remaining two people who stood out.

"I'll take the guy dressed up as Santa; you get the other one." Fake Santa's laugh, to Clara's practiced ear, held a note of derision at odds with the amount of Christmas spirit pouring off him. She'd have laid a crisp hundred dollar bill on him being the culprit if anyone had been taking bets.

The other suspect was a twenty-something looking girl with a mane of curly dark hair falling over the collar of a hand-knitted sweater in a white snowflake pattern scattered over an ice-blue background. Shorter than most of the adults, but taller than the children, she flitted in and out of the crowd without speaking to anyone.

"Deal." Mag chortled, and without further ado, the sisters filed back into the main hall to track their quarry. Clara made a beeline for Santa while Mag ambled in the direction snowflake sweater girl had gone.

"Excuse me, might I..."

"Out of the way, lady. I got something I gotta do." Fake Santa dodged past Clara and lurched toward the side door while her heart thundered in her chest. He must be guilty if he was trying to make a break for it, but how had he figured out she was onto him?

"Stop." Power sizzled up from the source of Clara's magic, from the place in her center that owed everything to the mighty Balefire from which she took her name. The command scorched the air between her mouth and where it landed on the cheap fuzzy back of his red coat.

Santa stopped so fast his top half continued on a pace longer than his feet had carried him and he over-balanced to land on in a heap on the floor. People rushed to cluster around the fallen man, but Clara was already on her knees beside him.

"What happened?" The muffled question came out from behind a beard that had been knocked askew in the fall. Wannabe Santa ripped off his stocking cap, yanked the elastic band off over his head, and spit out strands of fluffy white. Annoyed, he tossed the beard and hat away and turned his face toward Clara. Bald and wearing makeup to simulate rosy cheeks, the man didn't seem like much of a threat.

"Why were you leaving in such a hurry?"

"Look, I just need to go to the can. Some kid peed on my leg, and I gotta clean up the suit. It's rented."

Squinting, Clara took stock of the Christmas spirit swirling around him. All of it came from the suit, none from the man. She'd made a mistake. Of course, she had. Hundreds of children speaking their Christmas wishes to the man in the faux fur would imbue the suit with enough spirit to be seen from space.

"Sorry. Here, let me help you." Clara braced herself

and yanked fake Santa to his feet before searching for her sister.

Despite Mag's assurances that her advanced age only went skin deep, her slower pace allowed Clara to catch up.

"Not Santa," Clara said as she rocketed around her sister to cannon into the back of the second suspect. No small woman, Clara's tender mercies nearly knocked the poor thing off her feet, and in the ensuing scuffle to get the younger woman righted, exposed the merest hint of a pointed ear lurking under the riot of hair.

"Oh, I am sorry. I didn't see you standing there. Are you all right?" Acting concerned, Clara grasped the woman's arm firmly and leaned down to make eye contact. "My name is Clara, and I'm such a klutz some-times. This is the second time I've knocked someone over in the last five minutes." While she prattled on, Mag had time to catch up.

"My sister is a hazard to herself and others. Allow me to apologize on her behalf. Are you hurt, Miss..."

"Jackie. Jackie Frost."

The name fit what little the elf had been able to say before he passed out.

"Miss Frost?" Solicitously leading Jackie Frost

toward a less populated area, Mag peppered her captive with questions.

"We're new in town. Have you lived here long? Did you help with the party? Everything looks so festive, and the people are so nice. It's nothing like the city where we used to live."

Clara held back a snort when her sister put on a voice to match the doddering exterior she displayed to the world. There's nothing more harmless than a little old lady with a cane. Unless that little old lady was Margaret Balefire, who possessed a keen intellect and a rare gift of magic that had been passed down through the family line. Jackie Frost didn't stand a chance.

"No, I'm not local. I'm just here for the party, and I need to..." Jackie started to turn away.

Fanning her face, Mag declared, "Oh my goodness! I'm feeling faint." She clutched onto Jackie's arm like a limpet. "Be a dear, won't you, and help me outside. It's so warm in here." When Jackie made a move to say no, Mag poured it on even harder, sagged at the knee, and nearly swooned. There was nothing else the young woman could do, she sighed and gave in to the need to help.

Keeping the smirk to herself as much as she could, Clara followed Mag and her unwitting captive toward the door. The second it closed behind them, Clara touched Mag's arm and disappeared the trio into thin air.

Back at the house, Hagatha's eyes widened as three women toppled to the floor at the foot of Evergreen's bed. She sprang into action as Jackie Frost shrieked and lunged for the door—as much as a woman with a walker can spring, that is. Hagatha let out a holler of her own and dropped a magic dampening spell right before two streaks of fur raced up the stairs, whirred into a man and a woman, and blocked Jackie's passage.

"Pye, Jinx! Your timing is exquisite. Get her over to that chair, quickly."

Jinx held Jackie's arms at her sides while Mag patted the woman down quickly and with an air of a police officer simply going about her duties, as though she frisked people for weapons every day.

"Ah ha!" Mag exclaimed, pulling a baseball-sized object from deep within the folds of Jackie's skirt. Crystal clear water magnified the red and green-clad figures encased in the glass ball set into a simple pedestal of polished ebony until a flurry of snow obscured them from view. Elven spirit glittered and glimmered among the flakes.

Panic-stricken, Jackie went wild, struggling against

her captors, "Give that back, it's mine!" She shrieked at a pitch that should have shattered the snow globe she was trying so hard to reclaim and lurched with enough gusto to break free of Jinx's hold.

Mag tucked the globe into the crook of her arm like a football, shifted from one foot to the other in a little hop-skip and then waited for Jackie to take the bait before lobbing the thing over her head to her sister. Clara, recalling her monkey-in-the-middle skills from when she and Mag were children, caught it deftly in one hand and prepared for Jackie to change course.

What she wasn't prepared for was a barrel roll of Donkey Kong proportions. Jackie plowed into Clara's knees, knocking her off balance, and the globe went flying into the air. In slow motion, everyone, including old Haggie, leaped to catch the coveted object, but they were all too late. Clara watched as it hit the wood plank floor and shattered into a million pieces.

"No!" Jackie screamed, her face contorted into one of pain rather than anger, and she used the moment of confusion to, with a mournful glance backward, whoosh through the door and down the stairs.

"Look," Clara drew the room's attention back to the floor, where a swirling ball of sparkling motes had begun to zing through the air toward Evergreen's translucent form.

The essence of holiday magic enveloped him in a ball of snow, lifting him off the bed and into the air where he spun around in a miniature blizzard that chilled the room to near-freezing. Pye and Jinx took their leave in a similar fashion to the first time they laid eyes on Evergreen, opting to chase after Jackie instead.

Evergreen's eyes popped open as the full force of his Christmas spirit was restored, and he sprung into action with newfound vigor.

"She's getting away. That wily little minx somehow escaped Santa's workshop. I suspect there's a traitor in our midst because she was locked up tight as a jack-in-the-box."

"I guess someone turned her crank," Hagatha dissolved into giggles of glee. The woman really did have the oddest sense of humor.

"Somewhere, someone is running around with a giant butterfly net, looking for that woman," Mag muttered under her breath to her sister, who nodded in agreement.

"Respect your elders, Margaret, or you'll receive nothing but a bundle of coal in your stocking this year." Evergreen chided. "Jackie Frost must be contained. She was the mastermind behind her twin brother, Jack Frost's plan to steal Christmas. We managed to foil him last year and capture her, and she's been held at the North Pole ever since. We were hoping to use her as bait for her brother, and the clock is ticking. Santa Claus is probably having a conniption right about now."

"Well, now that you're back to your old self, we'll just leave you to take care of things." Santa's problem wasn't coven business, and Mag saw no need to trouble herself further. She'd done her best by the elf and Clara wanted to be back in Port Harbor to spend the holiday with her granddaughter. So did Mag, for that matter.

Evergreen folded slim arms over his chest, tapped his jingle bell-tipped toe, fixed Mag with a withering stare.

"Do you really want to be the witch who stole Christmas?"

"Look here, you little..."

"Mag." Clara cut off what was sure to be an entertaining substitution for a nasty name. "We have to help him. Not just because it's Christmas, but because you know as well as I do where Jackie is going to end up. The party should be over by now, and Gertrude will be home alone. We can't just turn our backs on a coven member."

"I suppose."

"This is just so heartwarming." Clapping her hands together, Hagatha made it hard to tell if she was being sarcastic or not.

With the promise of assistance, Evergreen turned thoughtful, then flitted around the room muttering things like, "Ugh, artificial tinsel. That won't hold her. Plastic. This will never do." He tested most of the decorations and came up with nothing that satisfied his purist's soul. "Too bad the snow globe is broken, it would have worked a treat. I don't suppose you could fix it?" After making the rounds, he ended up back in front of Mag who thought about it for half a minute.

"It would be tricky."

"Pshaw." Scoffing, Hagatha merely directed a glance at the shards of glass littering the floor, and they whizzed back together good as new.

"Useful spell for someone about to open a shop. You mind teaching it to us sometime?" Clara's question earned her a wink from Hagatha. Having the old witch around might not be so bad after all.

"Now to turn it into a trap." This was Mag's field of expertise. "First we need the bait." The steady look she laid on Evergreen told him exactly what she was after.

"Okay, but just a little." Concentrating, he spun a

portion of Christmas spirit into a shimmering ball. Mag nodded to Clara who cast the ball into the snow globe with a flick of her wrist.

"And now, we make it sticky." Seeing the direction her sister was going, Clara pulled a piece of fudge out of her pocket. "Gertrude's candy cane and white chocolate. I snagged it while we were at the party. I think I might be addicted; it's so good." Quick as a wink, she stole a nibble off one corner then sent the candy hovering over the glowing globe. A swish of her wand turned the candy into a shower of sticky, clear liquid that coated the glass. "That should do it. It's like flypaper for rogue winter imps."

Clara carried the globe and Mag transported the elf when the two of them skimmed to Gertrude's house where the front door hung askew on its hinges. Crashing and banging noises provided more evidence that something was wrong inside.

"She's here all right." Evergreen's words slurred slightly. "This much spirit in one place is intoxicating."

"You stay out here, then. Can't have you falling down drunk in the middle of a sting operation." Clara shoved Evergreen into the midst of the plastic elves decorating the lawn. "No one will notice you there. I'm going in. Mag, you keep watch out here, if she tries to get away, blast her back inside."

Clara grasped the snow globe and vaulted onto the porch. Mag would only have slowed her down. She sidled along the wall to peer inside, and, happy with what she saw, gave her sister the high sign before disappearing through the door.

Inside, Jackie was rifling Gertrude's cabinets, tossing bottle after bottle of Christmas spirit into a bag. Clara crouched behind the sofa and gently, ever so gently, magicked the snow globe a little closer each time Jackie turned her back. Soon enough, she managed to settle the trap in place. Now it was a matter of waiting until her quarry took the bait.

Scanning the room Jackie's eyes alighted upon the trinket, and her hand closed over the glass globe at the precise instant she realized the object shouldn't have been there in the first place.

She let out a howl and tried to shake it free of her hand, but the fudge-coated exterior refused to budge. A clamor of hooves from the ceiling two stories above preceded the muffled slide of a robust belly rocketing down the chimney, and Jackie spouted a slew of profanities at Santa before being sucked into the globe with a pop and a thud.

"Tisk tisk, Jackie Frost, you've been a naughty girl this year." Santa tucked the globe away in the pocket of his velvet suit and turned to face the group assembled before him.

Evergreen leaped into his creator's arms and explained what had happened in a flurry of excitement.

"Yes, yes, my child, you did a wonderful job," Santa assured the elf kindly and with a wink over his head for Mag and Clara who were rudely shoved aside by a returning Gertrude.

"What happened?" The late arrival scanned the room with mounting surprise as she took in the assembled group. "Oh. An elf. A real live elf." She beamed and clapped her hands, but when she got a look at who owned the arms currently cradling the red and green clad figure.

"Santa," she breathed barely able to take it all in, and then her lips curled into a wicked smile as Mag and Clara sidled toward the freedom waiting outside.

"Oh my Goddess, you're really here!" Gertrude scurried into action, conjuring enough cookies and cocoa to feed the entire staff of Santa's workshop. "Please, have a snack before you go. Try the monkey bread and if you don't mind, I have a few questions."

QUICK AND EASY MONKEY BREAD

This is a pull apart bread, great for holidays.

INGREDIENTS

- 3 cans refrigerator biscuits, buttermilk
- 1 cup sugar
- 2 tbsp cinnamon
- 1 stick of butter
- 2 cup broken nuts (walnuts or pecans work best)

INSTRUCTIONS

1. Add sugar and cinnamon to a gallon sized freezer bag. Cut each biscuit into quarters and add to the sugar and cinnamon a handful at a time, shaking to coat each piece in the sugar and cinnamon mixture.

2. Layer coated biscuits in a Bundt pan, along with raisins and nuts.

3. Melt butter in a saucepan, add the brown sugar and bring just to a boil. Pour mixture over the biscuits, raisins, and nuts.

4. Bake at 350 degrees for 30 minutes. Cool before eating.

Vacation from Murder

A Mag & Clara Balefire Novella

Sand spewed as the old VW minibus lurched across the narrow curve of Pingree beach and shuddered to a halt inches from the damp remains of an ebbing tide. Behind the wheel, Clara Balefire breathed deeply of the salt-tanged air and took in the view from under the wide brim of a straw beach hat.

A black one, as befitted a witch of her age and stature.

"We're here." Her cheery lilt dropped into the rushing sound of waves coming through doors left open by her passengers in their haste to curl toes into warm sand. Closing down Balms and Bygones and bringing everyone here for a long weekend away had been the right choice.

Three days of sand and sun and sea. Sheer bliss.

Or a total nightmare with two sister witches and their mostly-feline familiars crammed into the back of a tin can on wheels. Totally worth it, though, if the

Balefires could spend a weekend not having to pretend to be something they weren't. Like mother and daughter rather than sisters, for instance.

Blood magic came with a few perks. Magic being the best of them, but the enhanced lifespan didn't suck, either. Unless you were Mag Balefire, who'd almost been killed battling a raythe. She'd escaped with her life, but lost most of her youthful good looks and agility.

"We need to unpack and set camp," Clara shouted toward the retreating backs of her sister and their familiars. When all she got in response was a dismissive hand wave, she flicked a whisper of magic to close the doors and reversed the van into a shaded spot among the towering pines above the beach line. Her sister and the two cats might be able to relax without having their campsite shipshape and ready, but Clara needed order before chaos.

Only grumbling a little about the work, she began emptying the contents of the van's cargo area. First order of business — set up the screened enclosure and the nifty picnic table that folded up into a plastic box. Gotta love modern technology, she thought.

She struggled through ten minutes of trying to deci-pher the instructions for setting up the screen house before discovering the problem. Some of the snap-together tubes carried the wrong stickers. She had eleven marked with the letter B and five Cs when there should have been eight of each.

"Bother." Looking both ways to be sure no one was watching, Clara held the image of the finished structure in her mind, called upon the power coiled inside her, and let magic take its course. Pieces and parts snapped into position to form the completed frame.

"I saw that." A dry voice came from the other side of the bus. "And I approve, little sister."

"Oh shut up." Clara snapped as she bent to unfold the plastic-coated canopy, then instantly regretted being churlish. This was supposed to be a fun vacation, not one riddled with more stress. "Grab the other end, or did you want me to ask Pyewacket because she's taller?"

Pye could morph into an Amazon-sized woman with smoky eyes, a long fall of sable hair, and tawny skin that looked like it had been kissed by the desert sun even in the dead of winter. But she preferred her native form: that of a sleek Siamese cat.

"I can manage." Gruff even when she was in a good mood, Mag Balefire, Clara's older sister, would not be outdone. Using more muscle than she appeared to possess, she tossed her half of the canopy over the frame and helped secure the ropes.

Without magic. Just to prove a point.

"Where are the camp chairs? Those ones I packed—the wooden ones with the canvas seats."

"You packed? I seem to remember you tossing stuff into the driveway and haranguing me to make sure I fit it all into the bus." Softening the comment with a smile, Clara realized it had been a long time since she'd seen her sister this excited about anything. Then again, getting away from people was Mag's idea of a good time, so it made sense that a deserted beach would be her happy place.

Pingree certainly qualified as deserted. They'd had to scout the place first, to make sure it was as remote as Mag had remembered, then cast a spell to make the VW drive on water to get there. The only other access route involved a mile-long hike on a barely used trail over moderate terrain.

Next time, Clara decided, it would be her turn to choose the vacation and they could take a cruise.

"Half this stuff is archaic. What is this even for?" She picked up a contraption that looked like it was made of nothing but metal arms.

In a tone that added the word 'idiot' to the end of

the sentence, Mag replied, "It's a stand." Then she grinned at Clara's annoyed glare.

Fighting to pry apart the accordion folds, Clara pinched her finger, uttered a dirty word, and handed the thing over to her sister. With practiced hands, Mag gave the rack a flip and it fell into place like an obedient dog.

"Holds the camp stove. You'll be thanking me in the morning when I fire up the old Coleman and make percolator coffee better than anything that comes out of that monstrosity of a drip machine. The beeping alone is enough to drive me buggy, and it makes barely passable coffee besides."

Mag hated the coffeemaker, and she wasn't fond of the toaster, either. It beeped three times when she pushed the handle to lower the bread into the machine. Why? Was it made to wake up people who made toast in their sleep? Or for people who weren't aware of what their hands were doing? Then it beeped again when the toast was done.

Modern technology, what a load of crap. Except for the washing machine and the television. Those she liked.

The camp stove looked like a metal suitcase and was so old the hinges creaked when Mag nudged it open and placed it on the folding legs. Once she'd connected the propane by means of a flexible hose and flipped the knob, the burner lit with only a tiny spark of Balefire she conjured on the tip of her finger.

"See that? Works like a charm. Just because something is old doesn't mean it should be put on a shelf." In a rare bout of philosophical thinking, Mag mused, "Kills the soul of a thing to go unused."

Was she talking about herself?

The moment passed while the sisters continued setting up their weekend getaway. Mag's familiar, Jinx, shook off fluffy white fur in favor of his human shape to help blow up a pair of air mattresses for the rear cargo space of the minibus.

"Remind me again why we're doing this the hard way." Jinx seemed more interested in stretching out on a sun-warmed rock and toasting his fur as a cat than treading away on the foot pump.

Witches of uncommon power and ability, the Balefires could conjure up a magazine-worthy camping experience without waving a wand. But what would be the fun in that?

"You'd be missing out on the—" Mag started and Clara chimed in, "—whole camping experience."

"I've got nothing against camping; I just didn't

realize we were going to be doing it fifties-style." In a rare moment of unity, Pye sided with Jinx. As different as night and day in personality, the two rarely agreed on anything.

"It's not supposed to be a weekend at the Ritz," Mag said. "Camping is all about the simple things, and getting back to nature. Roughing it in the woods. Us against the elements, living by our wits, and the bounty we can pull from the bosom of Mother Nature."

A pop and a luffing sound interrupted her preaching on the subject, and Jinx said, "Uh oh."

The mattress whistled as it deflated.

"Let's leave Mother Nature's boobs out of it, okay?" Getting back to nature was one thing; it being all up in her personal business, Clara thought, was quite another. "I think there's a happy medium to be found somewhere between having a few of the creature comforts and spending the weekend eating bugs and using a rock for a pillow."

To that end, she retrieved her purse and dug around to find an item with no sharp edges and small enough to fit through the air inlet.

A master at making charms, Clara preferred using found or recycled materials. The bottom of her handbag carried a more eclectic jumble of items than a young boy's pockets. Among the lint, she found three or four plastic beads. How long they'd been rolling around in there, she couldn't say, but, infused with magic and directed by her intent, they'd provide protection from further punctures.

That job done, she slipped a protective charm through the hole and applied the patch kit so thought-fully supplied by the mattress people. Fortunately, they'd foreseen this precise circumstance.

Clara also let Jinx off the hook and took care of the second, twin-sized air mattress. Seeing the speed with which the first had deflated, and knowing how sharp Pyewacket's claws were, she doubled up on the charms and whispered a spell to power up the pump.

"Don't know why you spent good money on those bits of plastic when I had a nice set of canvas cots we could have used."

"Nice?" Clara snorted. "One was missing two inches off one leg and moths flew out of the other one when I picked it up."

Mag sputtered and coughed something that sounded like *sissy* under her breath, but come morning when her bones didn't ache, she'd be grateful for sleeping on air instead of the hard bus floor.

Another flick of magic and the interior of the van

adjusted to fit the beds with some space between them. Sisterly love did not involve sleeping in the same bed with Madame Snores-a-lot, and Clara had every intention of tossing a sound deadening charm at the first snort.

"Fancy a walk on the beach?" With a final appraising look, Clara determined the site was ship-shape enough to warrant a break.

Pyewacket exchanged a wary look with her feline counterpart and shook her head vehemently, "I have no desire to feel the waves crashing against my ankles."

"Vacation doesn't mean 'a chance to exercise.' I'm with Pye on this one. We'll find ourselves a nice place to nap along the way, and you two can act as shark bait."

Mag rolled her eyes, "We'll see how you feel when I'm putting together a clambake later. Wimps."

Slightly mollified, and even more intrigued by the mention of clams, the two whirled into their cat forms and trotted on ahead, while Mag leaned on her cane and led Clara toward a gap in the tree line that opened onto a stretch of pristine white beach.

Rocky crags flanked both ends of the expanse, creating a natural barrier from the rougher waters on either side. In the sheltered inlet, waves crashed lightly along the shore.

A light, salty wind whipped Clara's mane of chestnut hair around her head as she lifted her face to bask in the sun's warm glow. "This was an excellent choice." She stated her earlier thought out loud, giving Mag credit for having sifted through a dozen options before settling on Pingree Beach.

"I'll show you another reason I chose this particular spot." Mag's voice held a glint of excitement as the pair approached a wooden sign planted in the sand. "Read the caption."

Clara squinted in the glare for a moment before uttering an incantation and conjuring a pair of sunglasses to rest on the bridge of her nose. "Pingree Beach, the resting place of the dreaded pirate Barnaby, is steeped in mystery and intrigue. Legend says that somewhere on this beach lies a hidden treasure trove of gold and jewels, buried by Barnaby before he was betrayed and murdered by his own crew. Many have tried, but all have failed, to find the missing bounty, but every year Pingree Beach is visited by hopeful treasure hunters who still believe the tale."

Mag grinned like a schoolgirl, her expression so innocently giddy Clara couldn't help but smile.

"We're going to hunt for that treasure, and we're going to be the ones to finally discover it!" Mag vowed, continuing down the beach while holding her cane out in front of her and tapping it against the sand. It wouldn't have surprised Clara one bit to learn Mag had put a metal-detecting charm on the thing.

If there even *was* a real pirate Barnaby. Clara doubted he had ever set one foot on this beach. Finding his treasure seemed unlikely, but she knew better than to tempt fate and speak her mind on the subject. Mag could pull off a miracle and she'd never hear the end of it.

TWO

"Kaeden, give it back. *Right now.*" The voice of a child attempting to be quiet but not quite succeeding woke Clara from a dead sleep.

"No, I'm the one who found it. Finders keepers, losers weepers." The boy named Kaeden hissed back, his lisp causing the words to run together as though he were trying to talk with a mouth full of bubble gum. "Mom said."

The first boy huffed and lowered his voice another octave. "I don't care what Mom says, and don't you dare tattle on me or I'll find a cave to leave that stupid stuffed elephant in, and you'll never see Jerry again."

Kaeden's voice cracked and Clara could tell he was about to let loose the waterworks. "You're a jerk, Xavier. Go find your own shell. There's tons of them on the beach. And don't you worry, Jerry," he said lovingly. "I won't let him leave you in a cave."

"Give it!" Xavier was starting to get annoyed.

"You'll have to catch me first!" Kaeden hollered and took off at a run.

At the exclamation, Mag shot straight up in bed, a flicker of Balefire ready at her fingertips.

"Relax, Maggie, it's just a couple of kids," Clara whispered. "They must be camping nearby."

Mag groaned, "You mean we've been invaded. Wonderful." Sarcasm colored her tone as she spat the last word.

The commotion awakened the familiars, and Jinx, hidden behind the curtains lining the VW's windows, transformed into his human form and took over the role of complainer. "We'll be the ones to suffer, you know. Kids always pull on our tails and rub our fur in the wrong direction."

"Quit your bellyaching." Clara admonished, brushing off Jinx's concern and leveling Pyewacket with a gaze before she had a chance to add anything. "There's nothing to do now except introduce ourselves. We don't want it to be awkward."

She swung the back door of the minibus open, stepped out into the warm morning breeze, and made a beeline for the next site over where a harried-looking couple attempted to pitch a tent. Clara couldn't help but raise an eyebrow as she approached and caught a snippet of their conversation.

"It's just a couple of days, Renee. Give the boys a chance to roam free for a change, and enjoy the peace and quiet. Dr. Hopper recommended more time bonding as a family, and there aren't any distractions out here." The man's voice remained even and his tone neutral, though Clara could practically see the waves of tension rolling off him.

Their body language—his hunched shoulders and the way she kept her body turned slightly away—told Clara plenty.

Renee took a deep breath and sighed. "Okay, Tim, I'll accept we had to come to the back of beyond with nothing more than we could carry on our backs. But I'm telling you right now, if I see one single wood spider, I'm out of here. Those things are pure evil."

Clara gave fair warning by stomping on, and snapping, a few twigs as she made her way across the narrow piece of forest separating the two sites.

"Hello, there. I just wanted to come introduce myself. I'm Clara, and I'm camping just over there with my mother, Margaret." She pointed toward the VW, where Jinx peeked his whiskers out from behind one of the curtains and evaluated the new arrivals.

"Nice to meet you, Clara," the woman said. "I'm Renee Young, and this is my husband, Tim. Our boys, Xavier and Kaeden, are around here somewhere. They're nine and eleven and can be quite a handful. Just let us know if they get on your nerves." Renee extended a hand, and Clara shook it politely.

"Really, they're no trouble at all," Clara replied lightly. Mag probably wouldn't throw an actual curse at her for not banning the children from their designated area.

"Enjoy your weekend, and let us know if you need anything," Clara offered before taking her leave and returning to where Mag was busy measuring grounds for a pot of her celebrated percolator coffee. She raised an eyebrow as Clara settled into a folding chair.

"They're perfectly nice, and I think they have enough to worry about. I got the distinct scent of a last-ditch effort to rejuvenate a relationship."

Mag snorted, "Well, in that case, they should have brought a bigger tent."

"Or a smaller sleeping bag."

. . .

"Why did you bring your cats camping? Don't cats hate the water? Are you afraid they'll run off and drown? Do you think it's going to rain tonight? The sky looks kind of dark and gloomy. Did I show you my elephant? His name is Jerry. His wife, Jasmine, is at home. They're taking a break." Kaeden talked a blue streak while following Mag around the side of the minibus, which, upon seeing the interior, he'd deemed 'the awesomest camper ever.'

Xavier, who was considerably more gentle with the cats than Clara would have expected after hearing the way he spoke to his brother, had coaxed Pyewacket out of hiding with a piece of beef jerky pulled from the depths of a bulging cargo pocket. Now she was curled up on his lap, purring gently while he scratched the silky spot behind her ears.

Which one enjoyed the experience more, Clara couldn't tell.

"You can tell him to shut up if you want to. It won't help, though. He never stops talking." Xavier commented with an eye roll.

Clara grinned. "I have a sister who does the same

thing." She said, her eyes twinkling as they met Mag's. "What grade are you in, Xavier?"

"I'll be in sixth this year. That's middle school. So much cooler than elementary." His voice held pride and a little bit of trepidation, not that he'd admit it, Clara was sure.

Kaeden continued his verbal assault on Mag until Jinx approached from the beach with a piece of white fabric in his mouth. "Hey, that's my sock!" He hurried over to the cat and tried to tug it away, but Jinx held on and then took off in the other direction, whiskers twitching in feline challenge.

Giggling, his chubby cheeks dimpled, Kaeden handed the beloved elephant to Mag and ran after Jinx.

The pair returned minutes later, with Kaeden carrying Jinx, and Jinx still carrying the sock.

"You'll never guess what I found. Not in a million, billion years." Sock forgotten, Kaeden lowered Jinx onto one of the folding chairs and bounced from one foot to the other in front of his brother.

Showing all the scorn he could muster, Xavier raised an eyebrow at his younger brother but declined to guess.

"A pirate buried his treasure right here on the beach."

"Did not."

"Did, too. Says so on one of those poster things. It's over there."

Rare is the boy, even one jaded by his place as the eldest brother, who can resist the lure of pirate booty. Not even one who has reached the lofty age of eleven.

"Here, take this, but don't forget to return it when you're done." Mag handed over the folding camp shovel she'd brought along in case she wanted to do a little digging herself.

"Thanks! I call first dibs." Xavier hastily dumped Pye off his lap, and, grabbing the shovel, followed his brother toward the beach.

"Sorry, Pye." Grinning at the annoyed arch of feline back, Mag qualified, "But I bought us some peace and quiet."

And Mag took advantage of both by plunking down in her chair for a nap.

"I'm worried about those kids. They must be miserable in that tent." In the rain-lashed darkness, Clara couldn't see any sign of light glowing through the canvas. She hoped the Young family had decided to hunker down and try to sleep through the storm.

The sound of the wind came first. Like a cornered animal, the growl and roar of it announced worse to follow, until the wall of air bashed against the side of the bus, rocking it until the springs creaked. A spatter of hail mixed with the driving rain pinged off the metal roof. If this kept up, no one would be getting any sleep.

Half an hour crawled past before Mag pulled out the Parcheesi board and talked the familiars into playing. Clara joined in, but with half her attention focused elsewhere, only managed to move one of her pieces home by the end of the game.

"Suck it, losers." As usual, Mag gave no quarter when a win was on the line.

"You don't have to rub it in," Jinx collapsed into his furry form and presented his backside to his witch companion. Mag retaliated with a snarky comment, and in return, a flick of his tail sent dice and markers scattering.

"That was rude." Still, Mag smirked at his retreating back.

"So was your victory dance." With an impatient flick, Clara's magic sent the game pieces sailing into the box. The constant whine of the wind grated on nerves already frayed. "Let Jinx pick the next game, but I reserve the right to veto."

Twenty pounds of fluffy cat hit the floor with a thump as Jinx made his way to the stack of games. He hesitated long enough for Mag to make an annoyed *hmphing* sound before he laid a white paw on Monopoly.

"Veto," Clara shook her head, "Takes too long. We'll be up all night. Pick again."

"Park and Shop," Pyewacket suggested.

"Veto." This time from Mag. "I'm on vacation from anything that has the word 'shop' in it."

Jinx let out a sound that was somewhere between a squeak and a snarl, then the paw landed on Clue. When no one opposed, he shook off his fur and returned to human form, muttering something about being surrounded by females.

The wind died down sometime before Clara outed Colonel Mustard for doing the dirty deed in the ballroom with a rope.

"Now that's more like it," she said as she settled down with the patter of a gentle rain lulling her to sleep.

The soft light of a morning sunbeam filtered through the window and played over Clara's face. Her eyes felt drier than Saharan pebbles covered in grit when she finally pried them open. Judging by the pesky beam's angle, she figured it couldn't be later than seven. Too early to get up on a day when she had nowhere else to be.

With a lazy finger twitch, she flicked the curtain closed and went back to sleep.

"You think they're all dead?" When a nine-year-old boy attempts to whisper, it rarely comes out quietly. "I heard Mom and Dad talking about some houses around here being robbed. Maybe the bad guys came along and..."

Clara assumed by the slurping sound he made, Kaeden had also run his finger across his throat to indicate brutal murder.

"What would robbers come here to steal? A bunch of old camping supplies? Nah, they're probably just sleeping. Old people need a lot of rest. We learned about it in health class." Xavier's sage reply poked a pretty big hole in Clara's ego.

At two hundred and fifty odd years, she supposed she did qualify as *old people*, but she thought she carried her age better than most and didn't look a day over forty. Okay, maybe forty-two, but still.

"Dad said they're squashed because there's no road," Kaeden spoke with the absolute conviction he was repeating a solemn truth.

"He did not. He said squatted. He said they must be

squatting because they couldn't have driven in here. Can't you get anything right?"

A gentle snort issued from Mag, and Clara glanced over to see her sister also awake and listening to the pile of disdain Xavier heaped on his brother.

"Well, I think they're nice and I don't think they're squashes or squishy squatters. You're just being mean."

"Whatever, Kaeden." A rustle signaled at least one of the boys had gone.

"Don't listen to him, Jerry. I bet they're my fairy godmothers and this is their magic bus." So quietly, his voice barely carried through the thin walls, Kaeden added, "Maybe they can fix mom and dad before they have to take a break like you and Jasmine." Then he, too, padded away from the Balefire campsite.

People like Clara, when confronted with a child in utter misery, respond with compassion and a need to protect. Feeling exactly the same, but wired a little differently, Mag exploded with quiet fury.

"Coming here was stupid, and now we're going to have to deal with that family."

"Margaret Balefire, if you're suggesting we do something to hurt those children, I'll—" Rising from the air mattress like an avenging angel, Clara prepared for battle.

Mouth hanging open, face creased from sleeping, hair looking like she'd snatched it off Einstein's head and then run it through the dryer on the fluff cycle, Mag fired up.

"Who said I wanted to hurt anyone? You really do think the worst of me sometimes, Clarie." Hurt rode Mag, dug heavy spurs into her sides at being misunderstood. "But I'm not wearing purple and shooting sparkles out of my wand in front of that kid. I don't care how sweet he is."

"Oh Maggie, I'm sorry. That was unforgivable. I don't know what I was thinking." Sincere, the apology came with a hug that Mag couldn't avoid in the small space. "You're the best one out of the two of us."

"So you keep saying." Mag mumbled as she exited the minibus and grabbed the shovel. "I'll be out on the beach if you feel the need to accuse me of anything else."

Clara sighed and watched Mag walk away, wondering if she'd ever get it right when it came to dealing with her sister.

THREE

"Mom! We need a cardboard box and some tape to make a chest. We found Barnaby's treasure." Amplified by the water, Kaeden's voice echoed off the rocky bluffs and killed Mag's plans for fishing in peace. "Mom! Where are you?"

"Hush up, now. I'm right here." Sunbathing on a striped beach towel, Renee raised up on her elbows and regarded her youngest son. "You'll have to use your backpacks and your imaginations."

"But Mooom! A backpack isn't a treasure chest. It has to be a box."

"Well, I don't have any boxes. We hiked in here, remember?" Renee's tone said the camping trip hadn't been her idea of fun. "With only what we could fit in our backpacks."

"Oh, right. I forgot. Can I ask Miss Clara for a box? Do you think she'd mind? I bet they have one." Not waiting for an answer, Kaeden's feet left divots in the sand as he scampered toward the VW ahead of his mother's warning not to bother the nice Balefire ladies.

"Too late," Mag muttered, but cheerfully. Still, she felt no remorse at leaving Clara to handle the situation while she shouldered her pole and headed toward the brook.

The Balefire magic came down through blood and was rooted in fire, but that didn't stop Mag from sensing the power that flowed through the water and beat in the heart of the earth. The pulse of it thrummed under her feet, and when the trout rose to take her hook, she felt the spark and flash of its life force.

Mudwitch.

Not as fancy a title as Keeper of the Sacred Flame, but one she'd cultivated by making an effort to strengthen her connection to the magic present in the earth and all living things. Clara had made a better Keeper than Mag ever would. The job came with too much human contact and not enough solitude, particularly at Beltane when every witch in a two-hundred-mile radius showed up to renew her connection to the Balefire.

Amid the pomp and circumstance of ritual came the

one thing Mag dreaded the most in all the world. The bane of her existence: idle chitchat.

She could wax poetic about the pregnant curve of a 19th-century brass spittoon or discuss the ideal handle length of a bed-warming pan. But she had no idea how to fake interest in some veritable stranger's day-to-day life. Nor did she care to bore them with hers.

Still, those two boys. Something about them had pierced right through the layers of indifference she wore like battle-scarred armor. Never a mother—and she wasn't sure anymore if that was by choice or circumstance—the immediate connection was something she'd never felt so strongly. Only a person made from ice or iron could withstand such bright and eager charm.

Trout and salmon haunted sun-dappled shallows before vanishing into deeper pools, but they were biting, and she caught her limit faster than expected. In fifteen minutes, barely enough time for the quiet rush of wind and water to settle her nerves, she was on her way back to camp.

"Any luck?" From the shade of a beach umbrella, Clara watched Kaeden and Xavier excitedly collecting items amid storm-tossed seaweed.

"Yeah, but it's not as much fun when they practically jump on the hook. No sport in it. I like the thrill of the catch." Mag's shoes landed a few feet down the beach when she kicked them off to curl her toes into the heated sand.

Across the way, Tim sat on a beach towel a few feet from his wife and watched his sons. Every so often, his eyes flicked toward Renee, who seemed more interested in her paperback book than her husband.

"He's miserable." When Clara caught Mag watching, she offered a quiet opinion. "He loves her. Anyone could see that by the way his attention stays focused on her."

"Maybe he should spare some for his surroundings," Mag replied.

She pointed to the silver dollar-sized crab making a beeline for the shadowed safety offered by the spot where Tim's shorts gaped away from his legs. The furtive movement caught Tim's eye and he let out a high-pitched yelp. What followed was proof a crab is better at crab-walking than a man. Scooting backward as fast as he could go on hands and feet, Tim dodged left and then right, but the crab was in its element and determined.

The commotion startled Renee, who lifted her head to watch and failed to hide an amused grin at her husband being terrorized by the tiny denizen of the sea. A genuine smile banished the pinched expression that had worn grooves around her mouth. The weight lifted, and her eyes sparkled.

"Ngyah!" Tim rose to do the crab-in-my-pants dance across the sand, and Renee let out a peal of silvery laughter just as the little creature finally shook loose and dropped back onto the beach. It scuttled away, leaving Tim staring after it, his breath coming in short gasps, and Renee giggling helplessly.

"That wasn't funny." Now that the worst of it was over, Tim directed scowling attention back to his wife. It took only a moment for his expression to change from annoyed to something closer to wistful, and then, infected by her easy laughter, he grinned. "Okay, maybe it was a little funny."

"They're going to be okay." Watching the couple share a moment unclouded by strife, Clara felt a little choked up. "If they can laugh together like that, they can work it out. Can't you see how much they love each other?"

"Don't get blinded by the stars in your eyes, Clarie. Love isn't always enough." It sounded like Mag was speaking from experience, but if she'd ever been in love, she hadn't seen fit to tell her sister about it. Clara's only inkling on the matter had come from seeing a carefully preserved flower her sister carried in her pack, and an occasional glimpse of the same wistful expression Tim had worn earlier.

When he settled back on the sand after checking the area to rule out another brush with rampaging wildlife, the distance between man and wife was halved.

Heat and the lulling shush of waves kissing the sand sent Clara into a meditative state, which lasted until ten pounds of annoyed cat landed on her lap and almost knocked the breath out of her.

"You've put on a little weight," she told Pyewacket, and received a blue-eyed death glare in response. It seemed cats didn't like that phrase any more than humans, especially cats who could be both. "Sorry. You're a gorgeous specimen. Perfect in every way. Now, what's up?"

Pyewacket put her paws on Clara's shoulders and used her eyes to draw attention toward the access trail leading off through the woods.

"What is it, girl? Did Timmy fall down a well?" The Lassie comparison earned Clara a warning scratch on the arm. "Sorry, I couldn't help myself." But when Pye jumped down and headed in the direction she'd indicated, Clara tapped Mag on the arm.

"Saddle up," she said when a bleary eye rolled her way.

"Something wrong?" Mag went from half asleep to fully alert at roughly the speed of a hummingbird's wing. Flickers of witchfire played miniature lightning across her fingertips. The excess energy crackled and hummed, and stood her hair on end.

"Pye seems to think there's something of interest happening near the access trail. I trust her judgment, but if it's another dead body, I'm going to pretend I didn't see it and go home. This is supposed to be a vacation."

Mag declined to comment, but her lips formed a straight line. If she had her way, she'd still be dreaming about running through a field of daisies without fear of her bum leg playing up.

As dreams went, it wouldn't make her top five—no man with oiled-up muscles wearing nothing but a pair of tiny shorts—but it hadn't sucked. And given the choice, she'd go back to it rather than traipse off through the woods looking for who-knows-what. Clara wondered what had happened to her sister's plan of treasure hunting; she'd spent the first two days on Pingree Beach doing little else but sleep and fish and eat.

"No rest for the wicked." Mag arched her back to release a few kinks and picked up the stick of driftwood she'd been using as a substitute for her regular cane ever since she'd found it on the beach. "We need to gather some kindling anyway. Got fish to fry tonight."

Pyewacket led them to the edge of the woods where Jinx waited and then pranced along beside him down the trail. Just a few yards in, the cats veered off the main path.

Signs of recent passage were clear enough, Mag thought, if you knew where to look for them. A broken branch, a smear of black where someone had stubbed out a cigarette on bare rock, moss scraped away from the spot where a shoe dragged over a log.

Her eagle eye picked out every detail, no matter how minor. More than a hundred years in pursuit of rogue magic hammered home the basics of tracking prey.

"Looks like Pye was right. Someone has been through here, and not too long ago, either." Mag's hunter instincts hadn't deserted her, they'd only gone dormant.

"Not that there's any reason for alarm," Clara said. "This is public land and even if few people remember this place anymore, there must be some visitors every year. It's probably nothing to worry about." She hoped not, anyway.

"Then why didn't they come down to the beach and say hello?" Mag asked, her eyes scanning the trail.

"How should I know?" But Clara couldn't think of a good reason. Her mind kept playing imagined footage of worst-case scenarios that all ended with bodies on the beach. Hers, Mag's, or most horrible of all, two small figures, faces gray with death. "I think your paranoia is rubbing off on me."

"It's only paranoia if they're not really out to get you."

"Nice sentiment. Should I embroider it on a pillow? Or we could make an appointment to have it tattooed on your backside if that works better for you." Pique and longer legs carried Clara right past her sister, so she was the one who reached the sheltered spot at the top of the bluff first.

One look and she figured she'd be eating crow along with her trout that night. More cigarette butts littered the ground. Enough to prove someone had spent a considerable amount of time overlooking their campsite.

Brushing past, Mag couldn't resist. "See, I told you."

"Go ahead and gloat," Clara replied without heat. "It could still be a coincidence."

"You know how much I hate it when you use that word, Clarie."

FOUR

As the sky darkened and rain clouds blew back in to leak a steady drizzle onto Pingree Beach, the Balefire witches found themselves in the screen tent, huddled around a folding card table, entertaining two children with enough energy to make Mag feel tired just looking at them.

"Boo-ya!" Kaeden exclaimed, a smug smile pressing dimples into his round face, "You're under the trap, Miss Mag. Time to meet your doom!" He cocked his index finger against his thumb, and with an exaggerated gesture flicked the makeshift lever. When the Mouse Trap game turned out to be missing the crank handle that ran the whole business, Clara had saved the day with a bit of ingenuity and some of the detritus rolling around the bottom of her purse.

Mag watched, mock concern covering her face as she played it up for the boy whose genuine enthusiasm touched her heart in all its hidden places. The plastic arm pulled back to the tension point, then let go, propelling the tiny boot forward with enough momentum to knock the bucket over and release the first shiny silver ball.

Back and forth down the zigzagged hill, the ball rolled until it fell onto the smooth, meandering track to tap the stick dangling below the diving board where another ball rested, ready to propel the little crouching man into the bucket. Except the stick only wiggled, and the little plastic man remained poised to jump. Kaeden exhaled his held breath in a huff, disappointment wrinkling his nose and wiping his face clear of mirth.

"Aww, I got gypped." His face crumpled.

Xavier threw an exasperated look at his brother, "Mom says you can't be a sore loser. It's unbeknowing."

"Unbecoming," Mag corrected absently, "And she's right. Failure is a stepping stone to success. Do you know how many times I've failed in my life? What makes you a winner is dusting yourself off, learning from the experience, and trying again."

Kaeden listened with rapt attention that would have irritated his mother had she been there. Why is it that children can't hear the words their parents repeat over and over, but when some stranger says the exact same thing they're like little sponges, soaking up information?

"I guess you're right," Kaeden relented, "but winning is much more funner than losing."

Mag winked at the little boy, "It sure is, kiddo."

The next turn at the crank fell to Xavier.

"Eat my stinky cheese," he taunted and gave the handle a spin. When the cage slid down to trap Clara's mouse, he collapsed back onto the old camp chair and the sound of tearing canvas filled the air. Fear chased the surprise from his face as, chair and all, he pitched over backward.

A vision, maybe even a premonition, of blond hair matted with blood rose behind Mag's eyes and she acted without thinking twice. Magic sizzled across the small space and set the boy on his feet as the chair crashed to the ground.

"What just happened?" Xavier looked to Clara for answers she wasn't sure she wanted to give. "Because something did." He would not be put off.

"It was magic." The wonderment in Kaeden's voice was only half of what pinged on Mag's heartstrings. Mostly, it was the hope. Hope that she was, indeed, a fairy godmother sent to make his wishes come true.

And now, she'd have to do her best to make it so. Dratted kids—this was why she preferred a solitary existence.

Nothing Mag or Clara said convinced Xavier he'd performed a feat of agility under duress, which left them with two options. Provide no confirmation and let things stand, or cast a memory spell which might have repercussions.

An hour later, the boys went back to their tent convinced they'd seen true magic.

"It's not like I intended to show them my magic, it just sort of happened." Mag defended herself when Clara shot her a look. "And really, I'm not surprised they caught on. Kids are a lot more intuitive than adults. I mean, the boogie man is real, but most parents chalk it up to their children having bad dreams."

"Funny, because the other day they were little invaders who were dead set on pulling kitten tails and ruining our vacation." Clara had to work double time to keep the smile off her face. Mag had done the thing she did best: she'd saved someone from harm. She'd broken the rule of not showing magic to mortals, but it wasn't a punishable offense. More like a guideline than a law.

And now, in true Maggie form, she'd deflect any praise that might be heaped on her shoulders. It was her pattern, and the least Clara could do was give her the opening.

Mag cocked a hip, realized given the condition of

said hip, it was a bad idea, and settled instead for placing her hands on both of them before fixing her sister with a withering glare, "You really do know how to poop on my parade, don't you, Clarie?"

She raised her voice into a falsetto and proceeded to mock her sister, "Be less cranky, Maggie. Stop being such a sourpuss, Maggie. Stop wasting time looking for Barnaby's treasure, it's just nonsense! Play with the kids. Don't show your magic to the kids. Maggie, why are you so difficult?"

Pacing back and forth, Mag's irritation spewed out in a deluge that covered how scared she'd been when she saw that boy's head broken and bleeding.

"I don't know why Clarie. Maybe, just maybe, it's because you're an insufferable nag who can never just go with the flow. Be a cork on the waves every once in a while, for crying out loud, or you're going to drive me completely bat-crap crazy!"

"You did an amazing thing, you know," Clara shot back. "I'm proud of you, but why is it okay for you to be a cranky and cantankerous control freak, and when I call you on it I'm Satan in a Sunday hat?"

Mag raised an eyebrow and grinned, "Because I know when to let it go, and you don't." A completely false statement and she knew it.

Clara was probably the only companion Mag would ever have, and as much as she liked to goad her sister, she knew deep down that they only butted heads because they knew they could spew at one another all the livelong day and then drop the malice like it never happened to begin with.

The outburst had settled Mag's nerves, which was exactly what Clara intended.

"Come on, Clarie. There's no harm done, really. They're children with a story no one will believe."

"To be perfectly honest, I find that more than a little bit sad."

Dense fog obscured an early sky when Clara rolled over and banged her arm on the curved wall of the minibus. For the first morning since they'd parked here, no small voices whispered on the other side of the thin metal.

How had Renee managed to keep the boys quiet when talking was Kaeden's natural default?

A glance showed Mag was already up and out. Probably manning the percolator on the camp stove.

"They're gone." The bare statement greeted Clara as soon as her feet touched the mossy ground. "Lock, stock, and tent. Without so much as a goodbye. Maybe they told Renee about the magic and she dragged them out in the middle of the night."

Clara accepted the porcelain-coated tin cup of dark brew, sipped, and waited for the jolt to wake up her brain. Sure enough, there was an empty space where the Young family had been. Well, empty except for one of Kaeden's endless supply of balled-up socks abandoned near the cold campfire ring.

Jinx shot out of the minibus in a blur of white fur, pounced on the sock, tossed it into the air and when it landed, pounced on it again. With his ears laid back, and his eyes wide from the thrill of the game, he tossed and pounced, and tossed again until something made him pause.

Changing between forms with a shudder and a whoosh, human Jinx picked up the sock and turned it over in his hand. At a glance, it looked like the simple white cotton had been balled up from being carelessly yanked off a boy's foot.

"There's something tied into the toe." Working out the knot, damp now from a combination of dew and cat spit, Jinx finally tipped a sparkling tennis bracelet out into his hand.

"May I see that?" Sunlight glittered off the brilliant

cut jewels as Clara weighed the bracelet in her hand. "Those are real diamonds, feels like three carats. Maybe four. Looks expensive," was her initial conclusion, and she handed it over to Mag for a professional appraisal.

"It's vintage Cartier, and it's not a fake. See the stamp? You can tell by the clarity of the engraving. It's an older piece; there's some wear on the clasp. At first glance, I'd say it's worth somewhere between three and four grand."

Clara contemplated Kaeden's grimy sock while she tried to come up with a plausible reason for it to contain a diamond bracelet. "Frankly, I don't think that looks like Renee's style, and even if it is hers, this is a weird place for it to turn up."

"Look! There's—" Leaving the sentence unfinished, Jinx hunched and folded and sprouted fur, ran a few yards up the trail and shot into the air to land on another hunk of white cotton. Unable to help himself, he tossed the second sock around a few times, then set his teeth into the cloth to carry it back.

The sock had no more hit the ground when he raced off to return with yet a third. Sock number two yielded a pair of earrings, but the third was empty.

A stripe of fur stood up in stark relief down the line of Jinx's spine. His alarm was enough to convince Pye, who took feline form and stalked the perimeter of the former campsite.

Near the spot where the tent had been, she dived under a bush, pulled out a fuzzy, gray ball, and shuddered back to human form to hand Jerry the elephant to Clara.

"Kaeden wouldn't have left this behind."

Mag turned to Jinx. "Do your thing."

"Jinx has a thing?" He'd never shown Clara any indication of a thing, so this she had to see.

He turned his head to shoot her a look of utter disdain and she noticed his eyes, normally blue and wide, were now a glittering green and had refined in shape to a dangerous slant. A ripple passed over his fluffy exterior leaving behind a sleek, shining coat of fur draped on a muscled frame.

For a moment, he sat on his hunches as if considering an attack plan, and then he rose to prowl toward the beach. From the campsite, the sisters and Pye watched the flash of white as a series of long leaps took Jinx in a zigzag pattern across the sand.

"You didn't tell me he could go all Clark Kent like that." Impressed, Clara finally got a sense of the true partnership between Mag and her companion, but couldn't help thinking it was one more secret she hadn't been privy to before.

"You never asked." Worry kept Mag's smirk to little more than a fleeting twist of the lips. Senses once honed by dancing on the knife edge of danger roared back to life and she opened to them fully. It felt like welcoming home the prodigal son and was only slightly awkward because Clara stood watching.

Ill intent, and Mag could see it, lay over the campsite like a smear of dark smoke. The Young family had not left by choice. She'd bet her best wand on it. Not that she had her best wand in the pack she carried. Or any of her best hunting spells. Drat the safe and comfortable feeling of routine that had led to putting aside the tools of her former trade.

Energy spent in conjuring her tools now would be energy lost when it came time to use them. Better to move forward with what she had and trust her sister to make up the difference. If one Balefire witch could take on the worst witchkind had to offer, two of them were an invincible force.

Moving with panther-like speed and agility, Jinx returned from the beach and as he landed in front of her, flowed into human form, and handed over the fork he'd been carrying between his teeth.

"Found this on the beach along with a lot of boy-sized footprints and a few holes where they'd been digging. Suppose they found Barnaby's treasure and took off with it?"

"Unless Barnaby shopped at Tiffany, I'd say not. This is a rare set, though. Sterling silver, and worth a lot of money, but it's not old enough to have been part of a pirate's booty."

Kaeden and Xavier had spent half the day picking up "treasure" from the beach, and no one bothered to look at what they'd found.

Or maybe someone had.

Sifting through the events of the weekend, Mag remembered a pile of cigarette butts and a hushed conversation between two boys huddled outside the van. Her brain examined the events, turning them this way and that until the puzzle clicked into place. "They found the loot from the rash of summer house thefts."

The blood drained from Clara's face. "Then they're in danger, and we have to find them."

"Is that another one up ahead?" A flutter of white hardly showed against a carpet of pale moss. "There have been too many of them, which means those smart little cookies left us a trail to follow." Mag took the sock from Jinx while Pye prowled on ahead. As eager as their witch companions to see the children safe, the familiars were playing bloodhound for the day.

Jinx had even let Mag darken his fur with a handful of ash so he wouldn't stand out as starkly against the browns and forest greens. Not that Mag or Clara blended, mind you, but a pair of silencing charms went a good way toward hiding their progress.

Voicing the concern uppermost in both their minds, Clara said, "The parking area is in the opposite direction, and if they keep to this trail, they're headed toward the cliffs to the south. A perfect place to stage a tragic accident."

"Then we have to hurry and hope we are not too

late," Mag said, pushing herself to move faster than her bum hip usually allowed. "If anything happens to those boys, I'll never forgive myself."

For once, Clara agreed with her sister's melodramatic take on the situation.

Pyewacket surged on, her nose twitching as she picked up the scent and led the foursome onward and upward, toward the craggy peaks of the bluffs overlooking the ocean. Clara shivered as her mind sifted through a list of possible outcomes, each more gut-wrenching than the last.

Finally, as the sun slid toward the top of the sky, the troupe cleared the last wisps of fog, approached the final summit, and stopped short at Pyewacket's hissed warning. Her fur stood on end, and her tail puffed out to three times its normal size. Raised voices signaled the end of their hike, and Mag's danger meter began to ding.

"Tell us where you hid the rest of the stuff and I won't have to tell Bob to drop your parents off this cliff." A menacing male voice cut through the air, eliciting a gasp and whimper from Kaeden, whose chubby ankle was visible around the corner of the boulder from where Mag and Clara crouched. Barefoot, his feet were caked with dirt and bits of dried blood from where they'd scraped against jagged rocks on his way up the hill.

Mag stuck her head a bit further out and took in the scene before her. Xavier huddled near Kaeden, a protective arm around his little brother, his face arranged in a brave expression while his eyes fixed on something out of Mag's line of sight.

Behind the children, a second figure paced, his hand firmly planted on a large bowie knife dangling from his belt. "I think they need a little incentive, George." When Bob stepped forward and turned his attention to what was happening on the other side of the boulder, Mag caught Kaeden's eye and sent up a silent prayer to the Goddess that he wouldn't give away their presence to anyone other than his brother.

Wisely, the little boy maintained a straight face while poking Xavier lightly in the ribs and pointing toward the witches. Xavier's eyes quickly flitted to something behind and above himself and Kaeden, and then flicked his fingers pointedly in the direction Mag and Clara couldn't see.

"We need to be able to tell what's going on," Clara whispered, pulling a wad of items from her pocket as the two men continued to threaten bodily harm. She spread a crumpled Yahtzee score sheet against the side of the boulder and motioned to Mag, who recognized this trick from their childhood and searched her fanny pack for a jar of castor oil. When one didn't turn up fast enough, she went with the next best option and yanked out a bottle of clear nail polish from the pack around her waist.

Clara unscrewed the cap and dumped the liquid onto the paper, spreading it with the little brush as quickly as she could. Once covered, Clara lifted the wet score sheet back against the rock and uttered a spell for clarity. Immediately, the paper turned crystal clear, along with the rock and earth behind it, creating a peephole that illuminated what was happening on the other side.

Renee and Tim huddled in a mirror image of their children, their eyes darting back and forth between their children and the armed Bob and George. Renee's eyes were wide with terror, but Tim's lit with the fire of a man watching helplessly while another person threatens his family: blind hatred and intent to inflict some bodily harm of his own playing clearly across his features.

Suddenly, Xavier's flicking finger made complete sense. It was the same gesture Kaeden used when he ticked the lever to initiate the sequence in Mouse Trap.

Mag looked up.

If she applied a little magic, the makings of a crude trap hovered just above where the boys were seated, and she spied a piece of flat wood resting on the point of a rock close to the edge of the cliff. If Mag had to guess, she'd have said it had been left there by a pair of young boys fascinated by all the things boys should enjoy: pirates, treasure, and board games.

And if she'd had time to think about it, Mag would have noted the irony of the situation. Instead, she formulated a plan. Under the cover of Clara's silencing charm, she quickly laid it out to Jinx, Pye, and her sister.

"You know what to do." Nodding, Pye scurried off on silent paws while Clara searched for the next item needed.

"This one will do, Maggie. It's definitely big enough and it's loose. All it needs is a good shove. Once Pyewacket positions that board to your specifications, anyway." Clara tried to remain positive, but all she could think about was what a shame it was to hold enough power to turn a pair of bumbling thieves into harmless bunnies, and not be able to use it when it counted.

Revealing magic to two children had been one thing, but letting four adults in on the existence of witches was unacceptable, even with lives on the line. Clara didn't make the rules; they'd been in place for centuries, and for good reason. Helping this family was probably a step over the line, but Clara knew she wouldn't be able to live with herself for the next hundred years if she sat around and did nothing.

Mag vowed to buy her sister a vat of butter pecan ice cream on the way home as thanks for the silencing charm that made it possible for her to send a lick of magic toward the rope attached to the limb of a maple tree.

When this was all over, she had a few stern words to say to the foolish daredevils for using such a thin line to swing out over the cliffs. The spell took hold, and the rope lengthened and slithered into the desired shape while Pyewacket ghosted around behind their backs so Tim and Renee wouldn't see her.

Her path took her dangerously close to the attackers' ankles where she waited for the right moment, then nudged the board to flip it like a seesaw. Dusky fur turning him into a moving shadow, Jinx oozed into place, and Pye moved to her next battle station.

With a whispered signal, the plan went into motion. Clara pushed with all her might on the two-foot-diameter boulder she'd selected, and watched it all unfold. The boulder slid down a natural slope in the surrounding rock, making a noise more distracting than nails on a chalkboard.

"What the—" Was all George had time to utter before the boulder crashed onto the upended side of Pye's board, launching a crouching Jinx into his face, claws unsheathed.

He staggered around, trying to pull a snarling, hissing ball of fur off his face, while Bob stared in dumbfounded horror and forgot how to use his knife.

"Over here, dummy! Eat my stinky cheese!" Xavier pushed Kaeden out of the way and taunted Bob, who fell for the ruse hook, line, and sinker.

"I'm gonna—" Bob lunged toward Xavier, who dodged left at the most opportune moment. Hidden in the canopy of maple leaves, Pye flashed from cat to human, sliced at the knot with Clara's pocketknife, and let the trap fall. As the cage of knotted rope dropped over Bob's head and shoulders, Pye let out a triumphant yowl.

A slew of curse words followed Bob's capture and went completely ignored as Mag and Clara rushed to rescue Jinx and secure George with the help of Tim, who had used the moment of chaos to grab the knife that had fallen from Bob's hand. He tied George's hands behind his back and secured him to the closest tree before drawing back and punching the man square in the nose.

"See, Xavier, I told you they were fairy godmothers," Kaeden whispered loudly enough for Mag to hear him. The sentiment drew a smile from her lips.

Xavier sighed. "I'm never going to hear the end of this, am I?" But his voice shook just a little, and he kept one hand on Kaeden's shoulder protectively.

"Eat my stinky cheese?" Dimples winking, Kaeden announced, "That's going to be my new favorite phrase."

"Are you sure you're all right?" Tim asked, checking his family over for the hundredth time since the police had arrived and dragged George and his accomplice away in handcuffs.

"Could we have a moment?" Tim asked the uniformed officer who waited to escort the Young family back to where the boys had hidden the cache of stolen goods.

Noting the protective arm Tim kept around his

wife's shoulders and the way she clung to him, Clara figured they'd patched things up.

It was too bad it had taken a tragedy to bring the pair back together, but the end result was what mattered. And now they'd have something to look back on during hard times, a touchstone that Clara had a feeling would always bring them back to the importance of family. Whatever they had gone through, it couldn't be worse than almost being murdered by a pair of petty thieves.

Renee pulled away from Tim and approached the Balefire sisters. "I don't know how to thank you." She blubbered, before bursting into tears and enveloping both women in a grateful hug.

Clara spoke a few soothing phrases until Renee calmed down and finally let them free of her grasp. As soon as she had, they were in for another onslaught as Kaeden and Xavier decided to get in on the hug-fest.

Kaeden whispered something into Mag's ear that brought a genuine smile to her face, and she winked at him conspiratorially before pulling him into her chest and inhaling the scent of his hair. "You behave now. And you, young man, were very brave. You keep watch over your brother and don't ever take him for granted again, you hear?"

Xavier treated her to one of his signature eye rolls but smiled and accepted more affection from both women before returning to his family.

Pyewacket brushed against Xavier's legs, her little motor running at top speed, while Jinx leaped into Kaeden's arms for a quick goodbye cuddle.

If Clara heard Mag sniff once or twice on the way back to the minibus, she wisely kept her mouth shut. What was she going to say, anyway? Her throat felt a little tight, too.

"You ready to pack up?" she asked as they made it back to camp. "I could do with a shower and some food that didn't start out the day swimming."

"What's your hurry?" Mag asked, a sparkle in her eye. "Barnaby's treasure is still out there."

WICKED GIFT OF THE WITCH

A MAG & CLARA BALEFIRE NOVELLA

It wouldn't be Christmas in Harmony without three things: Gertrude Granger's over-the-top holiday display, Hagatha Crow creating some form of magical mayhem, and a group of carol singers from the next town over going door-to-door during the four nights before Christmas Eve. This year was no exception.

Still riding the high of actually meeting Santa the year before, Gertrude had outdone herself, and that was saying something. The magically powered glow from her lighting display turned night to day for half a block and triggered a power company investigation into why her bill didn't rise. She had to charm a dozen cookies with a forget spell to get the meter reader off her back and keep from disappointing hundreds of people who found a reason to wander past her house sometime between Halloween and Valentine's Day—Gertrude ran her celebration longer than most.

For the first time, Francine Shaw wouldn't be

among them. In fact, as she sat in her dimly lit living room with an unread book in her hand, Frannie wished the holidays would pass her quickly by. And that was why, when she heard the bright sound of carolers singing next door, she quietly reached out and turned off the one small lamp burning next to her chair. At least they'd shown up on the first night, so she wouldn't have to worry about them again.

"There," she spoke into the gloom, "That should do it."

Frannie might have been right if not for the addition of a hunched-over woman leaning on a tennis ball-footed walker bringing up the rear of the group. If anyone had asked the other carolers, none of them would admit to inviting Hagatha Crow to join in the singing. What's more, at the end of the night, none would even remember her being there. Hagatha had that effect on non-magical people—by choice. She found it far easier to work her magical mischief without worrying about anyone pointing the finger in her direction.

Hagatha didn't understand how regular mortals could get themselves into such a state of giddiness over Christmas. Probably some form of mass hysteria brought on by the inherent magic of the season.

"Give them even the barest taste of power," she said to no one in particular, "and they go overboard."

If you told Hagatha her opinions on the ways of non-magical mortals smacked of bias and ignorance, she'd have laughed in your face—right before she hexed you six ways to Sunday. Hagatha considered herself an equal opportunity pain in the butt and didn't hesitate to bedevil those of her magical community should the occasion arise.

Almost older than dirt, and the last of her family, Hagatha took less pleasure at Yuletide with every passing decade. She still enjoyed reciting the traditional spells and reading the omens for the coming year. Hanging holly and mistletoe over each threshold and above the fireplace for protection made her feel safe. But after too many years to count, even stirring the pudding clockwise in the direction of the sun had lost its appeal.

And so, as always happened when Hagatha found herself bored, she took to the streets of Harmony looking for new and different ways to make mischief. Running across the carolers had seemed like an unparalleled opportunity, so Hagatha attached herself to the group, walked up the ramp to Frannie's barren porch, and waited for just the right moment to unleash havoc on the unsuspecting group.

How about a nice rash? A really itchy one that came on mid-song. That would be fun, she thought. Or better yet, she could spell them to all misremember the lyrics.

Holy Hecate, Hagatha decided, why limit myself to only one spell? No reason I can't do both. She began to build the curse in her head.

"It's sad. This house is so dark and dreary," one caroler said to another. "Not so much as a shred of tinsel in sight. The rest of the street looks so festive, too. Just being here is enough to sap some of the joy right out of the season."

"Pick a short song, then, so we can move on to the next house. That one looks cheery enough to make up for whatever Grinch lives in this one."

Meanwhile, inside the house, Frannie sat in darkness, ears closed to the song, heart closed to any joy the world had to offer. Grief choked her by the throat, making each breath a chore.

Though it had been more than two months, it still felt like only minutes ago she'd held her father's hand and watched him pass beyond this world. With his final breath, she'd come to know what it truly meant to be alone. He'd been her rock, her champion, and the last blood tie she'd had to another living soul.

Almost every moment since he'd gone, she envied her father for finding peace. If only, she thought, she could choose to simply spread her arms, close her eyes, and fall softly into that same gentle oblivion.

But such was not to be. Frannie gave in to the darkest thoughts, decided she would not try to put the pieces of her broken heart back together. Why should she bother when no one was left in the world to know or care? Not even at Christmas, a time she'd once loved.

What use did she have, after all, for singing and mirth, or decorations and packages wrapped in gaily colored paper? With no family left, who was there to share in the joy of the holiday?

This year, Frannie hated everything to do with Christmas.

Get off my porch, she thought toward the carolers. I wish you would go away and never come back. I wish Christmas would pass me by.

Wishes have power, any witch worth her salt will tell you the same. Wishes latch on to whatever magic they find handy, which makes them unreliable at best and downright dangerous when the source of power happens to be a witch with wicked tendencies. Had

Frannie known just such a witch stood on her front porch, she might have chosen a better time to make her wishes.

"John can play the trumpet." With a singing voice that sounded like a creaking gate, Hagatha butchered the second line of Oh Come All Ye Faithful. When the wishes tapped into the rising magic of the spell she planned for the carolers, they picked up a bit of her intention.

If you're going to wish for things, try not to do it if the magic to grant them comes from a witch who prefers mischief to mercy, and magic above all else. But that is not the moral of our story.

"Oblivius recuro!" Without thinking too much about it, Hagatha whispered a different spell from the itchy one she'd planned. In fact, she couldn't have said why she changed her mind because she didn't remember doing so.

There, she thought, that ought to mess up the caroler's plans quite nicely. She hung back when the group shuffled off to the next house and stood looking at the undecorated porch. To anyone with more than a withered raisin of compassion and a bit of fancy in their hearts, the porch might have looked sad stretched across the front of the house with nothing but an old rocking chair occupying the weathered floor.

Hagatha felt the wave of Frannie's hatred for Christmas as the fog of it settled over her, but not the underlying pain at its root. Whether her blind spot came from a refusal to examine her own loneliness or from Frannie's backfiring wishes was anyone's guess.

Hate Christmas, do you? She sent the thought toward the woman hiding behind the closed door. You haven't seen anything yet. In the far too many years she'd spent roaming around the mortal coil, Hagatha had learned one thing—well, she'd learned many things, but this one spoke to her wicked soul—people only hate the things they secretly want the most.

The woman lived in a house that looked like Scrooge's vacation home, and she hated Christmas. What better way to get under her skin than to give her an overload of holiday cheer? Hagatha knew just how to make it happen.

No one was more surprised—or dismayed —than Gertrude Granger when she noticed Hagatha skulking around the Santa's workshop section of her Christmas display the next morning.

"Well, hello, Hagatha. What can I do for you?" Gertrude stepped outside, looked both ways down the street to check for anything odd in her surroundings. Hagatha had a reputation for outlandish behavior, and it was always best to be prepared when she was around. Stories of the old witch bordered on legend, like the time she'd led a turkey parade through town—skyclad.

"Nothing. I was just inspecting the tinsel for...uh... quality control. You can't be too careful with this stuff." Reaching out, Hagatha tweaked a shred of glittery silver from the thick rope wound around the workshop's porch railing. Butter wouldn't melt in her mouth as she palmed the sparkling tuft, then slipped it into her pocket. "Real silver, I'd say. The genuine article. Am I right? What do you use on it to keep it polished to such a nice shine?"

It was no secret that Gertrude's favorite topic was anything to do with Christmas. Once convinced Hagatha meant no harm, she launched into a long-winded and detailed lecture on the history of tinsel made from precious metals that included a whole treatise on the proper care of same.

"I could give you my recipe for the anti-tarnish spell if you want." Once Gertrude warmed up to a subject, she could go all day without taking a breath.

Rarely did anyone get the better of Hagatha, but the sheer magnitude of Gertrude's verbal assault shocked the old witch into beating a hasty retreat. Well, as hasty a retreat as one can manage using a walker for support.

"That woman could talk the ears off a field of corn and still have breath left to blow out the candles on a cake." Hagatha stopped to catch her own breath and patted the pocket holding the scrap of tinsel she'd stolen. "She's not going to be happy with me later."

Talking to herself didn't seem at all an odd thing to do. Hagatha spent most of her time alone by choice, and who better to talk to than herself, anyway? Most of the other town witches bored her to tears with how they kowtowed to the non-magical community. What was the use of having powers if you never used them?

And, she thought, it was about time to shake things up a little, and she appreciated the chance to force Christmas on a grouch and rile Gertrude up at the same time. A most efficient use of her powers, if Hagatha did say so herself. Nothing like a good twofer.

To that end, she beefed up the warming spell that kept her toes toasty in winter months, and as she walked back to Frannie's, laid her own magic over the top of Gertrude's on the piece of tinsel.

"Inobservatus," Hagatha spoke the incantation, and while the spell didn't exactly make her invisible, it did stop people from noticing her as she made her way along the street and back to Frannie's front porch.

"Now, for a little fun." She wound the tinsel around the stubby end of a nail sticking out from one corner of the railing, stepped back, and lifting her arms as if conducting an orchestra, set the spell to working. If she gave it a little extra oomph, well, it was the holiday season after all. Go big or go home wasn't just Hagatha's motto. It was her creed.

The piece of tinsel twitched once, then twice. Hagatha gestured with spread palms and poured on the power. Her laugh held wicked mirth—emphasis on the wicked. "Go, baby, go."

One more twitch, and then the silvery rope twined and snaked around the rail, sprouting lights, bows, and sprigs of holly as it went. Large, plastic candy canes marched up the steps, lined themselves up alongside the porch railings, and as a final touch, a sparkling wreath bloomed on Frannie's door.

Over at Gertrude's house, Santa's workshop began to look a little bare.

Inside, Frannie sat at her kitchen table and stared at the ham sandwich she'd made but didn't want to eat. What was the point? Nothing tasted the same when flavored with loneliness. Nothing felt the same anymore. She couldn't stand the sound of her own chewing.

Once, long ago, Christmas brought the sounds of bright laughter. Of family and friends coming together to eat, drink, and be merry. But one by one, the older generation had gone. Each one taking a piece of tradition with them.

First, the aunt who always brought the rum balls and never shared the recipe. Then the uncle who played the piano, which still sat silent in the front room.

Oh, her mother had tried to keep the traditions

alive, to take up the slack, and when arthritis bent her fingers so she could no longer hold a spoon to stir, Frannie took on the task. Over the years, the guest list whittled itself down to just Frannie and her parents, and then Frannie and her father, and now, just Frannie.

What was the point of it all? With her husband gone and no children of her own, Christmas couldn't be over fast enough to suit her. By this time next year, maybe the echoes of what she'd lost would stop resonating through her mind, stop pinging at her heart. Or maybe she'd feel like this forever. Frannie couldn't see into the future, and even if she could, she didn't want to look in case what she saw would be more of the same.

No one was coming this year, no one was left to care but her, and Frannie just didn't anymore. She'd just as soon turn off the lights and sit in the dark until Christmas went away.

She no more than finished the thought when tinkling music broke the air, and Frannie stomped to the door, whipped it open to see where the sound was coming from.

"There, that ought to do it." Satisfied, Hagatha turned to walk away. Over one shoulder, she flicked one more burst of power to set the lights twinkling in time with the music. She made it as far as the end of the wheelchair ramp when the wave of Frannie's fury hit her. The old witch did her version of a happy dance—she shuffled her feet a little and shook her butt.

"I guess that kicked you right in the old, baggy Scrooge pants now, didn't it?"

Busy congratulating herself on a job well done, Hagatha magically whisked herself home where she planned to make a nice batch of cauldron stew and think up an even better trick to play the next day. And so, she missed the rest of the show when Frannie stepped out her front door.

"What in the world?" Frannie eyed the brightly decorated porch. As she did, the stern lines of her face softened slightly. The neighbor's two daughters, she decided, must have thought they were doing their good deed for the year. Bless their hearts; those girls had been good to her daddy, stopping by to hover next to the chair where he sat on the porch of an afternoon and regaling him with bright little stories about their day.

Those moments had been precious to him, especially during those last few months when his smiles were hard-won from the pain.

She ought to make a nice batch of cookies, Frannie thought, just a little Christmas treat for those two sweet souls. And, she admitted grudgingly, the porch did look nice. Her father would have smiled. Frannie almost did, but she stopped herself just in time.

When the carolers arrived on her porch for the second night in a row—courtesy of Hagatha's forget and return spell—Frannie left the light on even if she tried hard not to listen to the singing.

On the second day of what Hagatha considered the Great Scrooge Comeuppance, she geared up her walker and cast the waterproof and warming spell on her shoes. She'd spent half the night thinking up one dastardly spell after the other to throw at Frannie. In the wee hours of morning, she hit upon a plan that required no magic at all.

Very few people knew this about Hagatha, but the old witch had a soft spot for animals. People, she could do without as very few of them ever did anything interesting enough to be worthy of her time or attention. In animals, she found an endless source of entertainment.

For instance, a cat enjoyed a variety of moods and cared little for the desires of humans. As far as Hagatha was concerned, cats were very nearly perfect.

That is why, on her way to Frannie's, she detoured past a certain barn where a litter of tabbies had reached just the right age to be liberated from the tedium of fighting over splashes of milk and the occasional supper of freshly caught mouse.

Bold as brass, Hagatha walked right past farmer Hank Bascome as he applied balm to a sore udder. She settled down on a bale of hay at the back of the barn and tucked her knobby knees up under her to watch the kittens pounce and tumble.

The fattest of the four ambled off first to sprawl with its belly up and slept while the others batted each other over the stray bits of hay that were their only toys. The little ginger, Hagatha noted, was the fastest, but she lacked the fire to defend herself and came away from every battle empty-pawed.

And then there was the inky black bundle of spit and fury with the Halloween orange eyes.

"You'll do," Hagatha cooed, and when he striped her hand for having the audacity to pick him up, she practically purred. "You're perfect."

Before you start to feel bad for the rest of the kittens, you should know that three children and their baffled parents woke up on Christmas morning that year to find furry gifts under the tree. But that's another story for another time.

On this day, Hagatha lost a bit more skin as she tucked the black ball of fluff into the inside pocket of her coat, where the darkness and warmth promptly lulled the little beast to sleep until Frannie's house came into view.

The porch, Hagatha noted, remained decorated. Score one for me, she thought, as she stomped up the ramp and conjured up a few things she thought the kitten would need. It was bad enough to drop the unsuspecting beastie off without so much as a by your leave; she could at least provide a few creature comforts when she did.

"This will push that crotchety old bat right over the edge," she said with wicked glee. Had anyone reminded Hagatha that it takes one to know one, she'd have probably turned them into a toad.

Frannie sat at her kitchen table, contemplating a cookie on a plate, and wondering where the night had gone, for it certainly hadn't passed in any sort of restorative sleep. After the flurry of activity around baking cookies, boxing them up, and stuffing them into the mailbox next door, she'd lapsed back into empty despair.

Everywhere she looked, she saw reminders of loss.

The photo on the wall with Frannie in her wedding finery, flanked by her parents, beaming smiles on every face. Next to that one, a photo of her husband taken just days before the accident that took him from her. Her father's favorite chair. Her mother's sewing machine.

Maybe selling everything and moving home to care for her father had been a hasty decision, but she'd have done it all the same if given the chance again.

Mired in such thoughts, Frannie jumped when she heard hammering at the door.

"What in the world?" She rose and went to look.

Outside, as she heard Frannie's steps coming closer, Hagatha clapped her hands in anticipation and wiggled her hips as much as she could given the rigors of her advanced years.

"Doesn't he just look adorable," Hagatha had attached a pretty red ribbon to the kitten's collar and tied into a perky bow to make him look sweeter than his actual disposition. "You'll take him in thinking he's as sweet as he looks, and then get the surprise of a lifetime, you just wait and see."

Frannie heard none of that, saw no sign of Hagatha, only the kitten in the cardboard box who gazed up at her with orange eyes. Again, she stepped outside, looked up and down the empty street for a glimpse of whoever brought her such a gift.

If the tear in Frannie's eye melted so much as a fraction of Hagatha's resolve, the witch pretended otherwise as the kitten, blast his wretched soul, not only let himself be lifted gently from the box but purred like a little engine. Anyone else would have found the sight enchanting when the tiny beast rubbed his head against Frannie's chin and snuggled against her bosom as if he'd finally found the human of his dreams.

Hagatha's hip wiggle turned into a foot stomp as she watched her dirty deed go down in flames. Old Mrs. Scrooge wasn't supposed to enjoy her comeuppance, she was supposed to cower before the wonder of Hagatha's magic and then see the error of her ways. Skipping the cowering wasn't part of the plan.

While Frannie and her new friend went back inside, Hagatha took a seat on the rocking chair to revise her plan. She rocked and thought, thought and rocked. What else besides decorations and presents marked the season for humans?

Then it came to her. Food.

"Rain of fruitcake?" She mused. "No, too messy. Life-sized gingerbread men could be fun." She pictured the look on Frannie's face when a giant cookie showed up on her doorstep. "Probably get the coven all riled up, and then I'll have Mag Balefire breathing down my neck."

Of all the witches in the area, Mag was the only one Hagatha had come up against with enough magic to rival her own. If the younger witch hadn't been raised a Balefire, Haggie thought, and a stickler for the rules when it came to dealing with mortals, we could have had some fun.

"Better keep my head down on this one before she shows up to spoil my good time." Not that it had been much of a good time so far. The way Hagatha saw it, she'd scored only one point so far with the decorating, but the kitten debacle canceled it out.

Meanwhile, inside the house, Frannie went through the items Hagatha had so thoughtfully provided for the kitten's care. A litter box, a tufted pillow for sleeping, and some food.

"I guess we'll get along just fine so long as you don't scratch up the furniture," she said to the cat, who blinked and purred at her. The sound broke up the terrible silence in the house, and for the first time in the weeks and days since her terrible loss, Frannie truly smiled. Having another warm body around, even one as small as a scrap of kitten, made a difference in her outlook.

Had Hagatha known how big a difference, she might have popped a blood vessel at the way her trickery kept backfiring. But as I said before, wishes have minds of their own, and any born of Hagatha's magic were apt to run as wild as the east wind ahead of a storm.

As she rocked, an even better idea came to the witch. One that made her cackle with glee and rub her fingers together until a red balloon appeared between them. She fitted her mouth to the stem, and blew, mixing a spell in with the air, and then tied the stem off with a complicated knot. Next, she spun the red bubble between her hands and whispered another spell to coat its surface, making it lighter than air, and then let it go.

The balloon bobbed and swayed and rose high above the town. When she judged the time as right, Hagatha held up her left hand, index finger pointed, thumb lifted high to simulate a gun, and said, "Pow," as she pulled the trigger. The balloon popped, dispersing her spell in an arc above the town.

"Get ready for tomorrow, Christmas hater. You're really in for a show, then."

Her wicked deed done for the day, and this one was

foolproof if she did say so herself, Hagatha went on home where she spent the rest of the evening toasting her toes near the fire and occasionally giggling over what was to come.

Across town, Frannie ran her fingers through the inky silk behind the kitten's ears and listened to the carolers sing.

FOUR

The day before Christmas Eve dawned as the town of Harmony sat quiet under a dusting of fine snow and magic. Hagatha rose before first light, tossed a mug of pumpkin juice into the microwave—a great invention, right up there with the automatic clothes washing machine and the air popcorn popper. When it suited her, which was any time it made her life easier, she embraced technology. Not that she went nuts and brewed her potions in the gadget or anything. The cauldron hanging over her hearth doubled as a soup pot when she wasn't brewing up something else, but for that first morning cuppa, she'd go with speed over tradition.

Looking out the window, she reveled in the sparkle of white still drifting down in fitful sprinkles. The timing of the spurt of bad weather made for a perfect delivery system for her spell.

By the time she'd drained the last drop from her cup, the name Frannie Shaw had flitted through the thoughts of every person in Harmony who'd ever known her. Cookies, pies, fruitcakes, and in one case, an extra ham went into boxes to be dropped off at her house during the day.

To Hagatha, a parade of people in and out of her house sounded like pure torture, and she expected Frannie to feel the same. Nothing like dealing with a steady stream of well-wishers all day to chap the backside even if Frannie's bar might be set a little higher when it came to how many people were too many.

Giddy with the promise of magical mayhem, Hagatha shrugged on her coat and decided to forgo the walk to town in favor of being on the spot when the deluge began. Picturing the rocking chair on Frannie's front porch firmly in her mind, she shifted herself there by magic.

"Where'd you come from?" Little Tommy Barnett eyed Hagatha from the base of the wheelchair ramp Frannie had installed when her father could no longer walk to the car. "You just appeared like magic."

"You didn't see me," Hagatha cast a forget spell on the boy, shored up her don't-notice-me spell, and settled in to watch the fun as Tommy's mother balanced a box in one hand and took his with the other. Hagatha made a face at him as he passed right by her.

Not very mature, but she did as she pleased. Always had, always would.

"Go ahead, Tommy, knock on the door," his mother said since she didn't have a hand free to do it herself.

"Can I say Trick or Treat?"

"It's Christmas, not Halloween. Don't you remember what I told you? We're bringing Mrs. Shaw a nice fruitcake."

"But why?" Tommy wanted to know.

"Because..." His mother struggled to remember what had spurred the impulse. "Because she's all alone this year, and I thought she might not take the time to bake for herself. This is the season for giving."

Tommy looked at his mother dubiously, "I'd have rather had Trick or Treat." But he knocked on the door anyway.

"Tr...uh. Merry Christmas, Mrs. Shaw," He called out when it opened.

"What's all this?" Frannie looked down at Tommy and then back up at his mother, but she didn't invite them in.

"We brung you a fruitcake," Tommy answered first. "On account of you can't bake if you're alone in the house. It probably doesn't taste very good, though. My dad says fruitcake is dis—gisdusting, so maybe this is trick or treats after all, and you got tricked." When his mother gave his hand a brisk shake, the boy subsided.

"What Tommy means to say is I was thinking of you this morning."

Hagatha watched the box change hands, noted Frannie's carefully blank expression, and cackled softly to herself. "That's got your dander up, doesn't it?"

Unlike Dickens and his tale of three ghosts, Hagatha didn't give a toot on a tin whistle if her efforts led to Frannie gaining the holiday spirit. Far more entertainment value if she didn't.

"I suppose you'd like to come in." It wasn't exactly an invitation.

"Oh no, I really can't. I just wanted to drop this by and tell you we're thinking of you. If you need anything, you just call. Anytime."

People always say that Frannie thought. I bet she'd sing a new tune if I called her in the middle of the night just to chat. "Thank you," was all she said out loud. The decorations were one thing, the kitten she'd yet to name another, but uninvited guests, even those bearing baked goods, only made her feel more alone. What Hagatha took for the kind of indignant fury she'd been looking to provoke was nothing more than a thin layer of protective armor Frannie pulled on over her heart.

But Frannie's armor wasn't anything close to the protections Hagatha put in place every time she ventured out to work her terrible magic upon her neighbors. Underneath the wickedness, in a place she wouldn't admit existed, the old witch meant well at least some of the time. Bored, she might be. Lacking the filter most witches had to keep from creating bad karma, she certainly was.

Still, in her heart of hearts, Hagatha wasn't nearly as wicked as she thought she was. She sat silent and watched as the good citizens of Harmony flooded Frannie with loving care, their concern chipping away some of the grief and pain. No burden is too heavy when many hands help bear the load. What she saw touched the old witch.

"Hecate in a handbag," she muttered. "She didn't hate Christmas at all. I guess I'm the Scrooge."

Wishes made on the power of a wicked witch never turn out well, but underneath it all, Frannie's were also Christmas wishes, and those have plenty of magic of their own. It would take a powerful working to get Hagatha Crow to admit she'd done something wrong. The entire coven in Harmony and half the witches in the state would have fallen off their brooms at the mere notion she might be capable of doing so.

"I assume you've learned your lesson, then."

Hagatha jumped when Gertrude Granger's voice came out of the empty space beside the chair.

"How long have you been standing there?"

"Long enough," Gertrude said as she shivered into view. "To see true Christmas magic at work. You did a good thing."

"I did not." Hagatha squirmed in her seat. "You don't know anything about it."

Clad in red and green striped leggings under a frilly red dress with a white apron over the top, Gertrude looked like she should be sitting on a shelf somewhere rather than standing with her hands on her hips getting ready to read Hagatha the riot act.

"I know you took decorations from my place and put them up here. Looks nice, by the way. Not arranged quite the way I'd have done them, but I'm not mad at you."

Hagatha rolled her eyes. "Okay, I did do that, but I wasn't trying to be nice." She saw her reputation going down in flames.

"And then there was the kitten. That was a fantastic touch. So thoughtful."

"How did you know about that?"

Gertrude tilted her head but didn't answer.

"It was the meanest one in the litter," Hagatha muttered.

"But what you did today was just inspired. Frannie won't spend the holiday alone now, and it's all because of you. No matter what your intentions, you made a Christmas miracle for her."

Whatever retort Hagatha might have made got drowned out in a shuffle of feet as the carolers mounted the porch to sing their final song of the season. If they left feeling a little itchy in places...well, even at Christmas, some witches will always be wicked.

Thanks so much for reading! We hope you enjoyed these novellas and have fallen in love with the characters that live in our heads!

Keep reading for excerpts.

QUICK AUTHOR'S NOTE

If you didn't know, ReGina and Erin are a mother/daughter writing duo—which means we've somehow managed to mix family and work without losing our minds (most days). We're so in sync we literally finish each other's sentences, though we do sometimes butt heads over plot points. But, being best friends means we just laugh it off and move on!

Characters are one thing we hardly ever argue about. They become so real, they tell us what they want to do! And once she'd been reunited with her sister, Mag Balefire let us know pretty quickly that they had more stories to tell and she expected us to get it done. Since she's such fun to write, we didn't argue all that much and the Mag and Clara mysteries were born.

Anyway, if you've come this far with us and not decided we're complete and total whackadoodles...and especially if you have, we're offering a chance to sign up for our newsletters— the best place to get new release updates, sales notifications, and other fun content.

You can sign up for ReGina's newsletter and/or Erin's newsletter, and as a thank-you gift for hanging out with us, you'll also get a FREE novella that isn't available anywhere else. And of course, we promise not to SPAM your inbox!

Love, hugs, and happy reading,
ReGina & Erin

P.S. If you enjoyed this book, it would be great if you could leave a review or recommendation at your favorite store or GoodReads.

Your reviews help indie authors sell more books!

EXCERPT FROM A MATCH MADE IN SPELL

FATE WEAVER - BOOK ONE

Being wicked is a choice. At least I hope it is.

Most families try to hide their sins away from prying eyes; mine erected a statue to commemorate theirs. Okay, that's not entirely true.

Homicidal witches turn to stone, immediately and irrevocably. The murder of one of our own is the one crime for which, in our world, there is no redemption. I don't know who makes the rules; I only know it happened to my grandmother.

Nobody is sure exactly what went down that day, but when it was all over, my mother, Sylvana, was gone, presumed dead, leaving nothing behind but the charred mark of dark magic on the earth. Only the trees bore witness to the vile act that orphaned me.

However it happened, my walk to work every day took me right past a life-sized reminder of everything I never wanted to be. On the afternoon when everything began to change, I was running late to work, and my Nikes hit the pavement in speed-walker mode, so I only managed a handful of steps before something odd caught my eye. A flash of color blazed against the granite.

A blood red rose with thorns the size of a baby's thumb sent a flicker of ice up my spine and set the hairs on the back of my neck vibrating. A cloud of scent enticed me to lose myself in its sweet thrall, to test a finger against a petal to see if it was as soft as it looked.

As much as I preferred to ignore this particular piece of my history, Clara drew my eye every time I passed by. That rosebush hadn't been there the day before. Trust me; I'd have noticed considering it was a month and a half too early for the delicate petals to thrive.

Immortalized in stone, my grandmother stared balefully back at me. No artist would ever be that skilled with a hammer and chisel; tendrils of hair whipped by wind or fire were picked out in exquisite detail around the face that haunted my dreams. Feral eyes, fixed on something in the distance, pierced through the granite. The fierce grimace of concentration that curled back her lips couldn't hide that she had been a beautiful woman. No hooked nose or warts marred the perfection of her face.

Even if Clara Balefire *was* evil to the bone, they'd

been lovely bones. For that, at least, I was thankful, since those same bones had been handed down to me. It was uncanny how much I looked like her. Another fact I chose to try and ignore.

Anyone who knew Clara points out how we could have been twins. Funny how no one ever mentions my mother. Speak the name Sylvana Balefire and those witches quickly find a stain on their shirt to fuss with, or a reason to bolt for the nearest exit.

Not that I have a lot of contact with the witch community. Whether it's because they know something about why my wicked grandmother murdered her poor, innocent daughter or they don't, I've never been certain.

They're probably afraid my defect will rub off on them.

Powerful witchiness runs in my family. With a last name like Balefire, how could it not?

My mom called me Alexis, which means protector. Alexis Balefire. Protector of the ritual flame. It's a lot of name to carry, so I shortened it to Lexi. Alexis is a fighting goddess who wears armor, carries a shield, and wields a sword. Lexi is the cute girl next door who wears designer clothes, carries a purse, and wields a lipstick.

That's who I wanted to be; or, rather, that's who I was destined to be. Call me shallow if you must, but saving the world isn't on my to do list. I'll settle for saving people from the perils of loneliness, and at least I'll be able to sleep at night knowing I'm not in danger from any falling houses. Wicked witches never meet their ends in a calm and peaceful manner, of that I'm sure.

But Balefire isn't just my last name; it's also my responsibility. Don't laugh, but an ancient Balefire lights up the fireplace in my living room, and since I have no other family to speak of, it's my job to feed it enough magic to keep it burning. If the fire goes out, bad things will happen in the witch world. Crazy, right?

Only one problem, though. The powerful magic running in the blood of my family passed right over me and, barring a miracle, at midnight on my rapidly-approaching twenty-fifth birthday, my fate would be sealed.

Witch or no witch. Soon the decision would be final, and I had little hope of it turning out the way I wanted. Looking at it from the glass half-filled perspective, not getting my magic would take away the worry of following in my grandmother's wicked footsteps.

But who wants half a glass of anything?

And being wicked is a choice I'd never make. I hoped.

What little power I did have showed itself in a heightened sense of intuition—one that applied almost exclusively to interpersonal relationships. Which is just a fancy way of saying I'm a matchmaker with a particular proficiency for recognizing potential love connections when I see them.

With no other skills to my credit, I used my limited powers to open up FootSwept Matchmaking, where word of mouth gets me as much business as I can handle, and allows me to help people fall in love almost every day. Who wouldn't love a job like that?

My office sits on the corner of a tree-lined block of storefronts backed by a larger section of converted factory spaces. Fumbling in my purse for the keys, I glanced up at the broom and stars logo painted on the front window just above the slogan, *Get Swept Away*. A nod to witchery only those in my closest circle understand. Once the door slammed behind me, I fired up the coffee pot, then opened my battered day planner to check my schedule.

I know, I know, I was a busy business woman in the 21st century; you'd think my entire life would be uploaded onto the cloud, but I was still attached to paper and lists. Somehow, the act of tracing the words, pressing pen to paper and leaving a physical mark on the page helped turn my intentions into actions. I don't think anyone else would understand my system, but it worked for me.

Not more than two seconds after I had settled in at my desk with a mug of steaming coffee, the phone began to ring and didn't stop for the next two hours. Business tends to run fairly steadily, with spikes of increased activity around the holidays. Other than the week directly after Valentine's day, my schedule is rarely overwhelmed; but lately, it was as though the entire city had become lovelorn—and nobody seemed able to sort it out for themselves. Not that I was complaining—but I don't like to rush through my work, and an increase in demand meant I'd have to turn clients away if I couldn't fit them into my schedule.

I slugged the last half of my coffee in one swallow, made a face at the now-tepid brew, and when a client I didn't recognize stepped through the entryway, hit the button to send all calls straight to voicemail.

"Are you the..the one? The matchmaker." The harried woman asked in a tentative voice. Her eyes avoided meeting my gaze, and her cheeks blushed a delicate shade of crimson. She scanned the office for the trappings she expected to find. A computer and a camera set up to record a dating video. Finding neither, her eyes fixed back onto the edge of my desk.

"I am. My name is Lexi Balefire. Can I help you?" I used my most welcoming voice and moved from behind my desk to lean down for a bit of eye contact. Thinking she needed a less formal setting, I led her to a cluster of armchairs occupying one corner of the room.

She sighed and sat down. "Probably not, I'm completely hopeless!" A tear formed in the corner of her eye, and she looked down at her trembling hands. Blond hair hung limply halfway down her back, and she wasn't wearing a stitch of makeup. On one wrist rested a beautiful, engraved silver bracelet, and the sandals on her feet looked like quality leather to me—but the rest of her outfit was clearly composed of bargain bin pieces. Frugal and smart, my instincts screamed, but self-effacing to a fault.

"What's your name?" I asked gently.

"Oh, I'm sorry, how rude of me. I'm Mona. Mona Katz. It's nice to meet you, Lexi." Despite her obvious discomfiture, the grip of her handshake was firm and when she smiled, her face transformed into something lovely.

I smiled and returned the sentiment. "Now, tell

me your story," I invited. This was the most important part of my job. Listening to the client is what activates my...magic might be the wrong word, but I can't think of a better one unless it's intuition. Magical intuition.

"Well, I seem to just have the worst luck with men. Every one I've gone out with has some problem I think I can fix. They always start out nice but end up being jerks."

At least she'd come to that conclusion on her own. One less problem for me to solve.

"I know I'm not the whole package or anything; I'm just a plain-Jane pastry chef with a decent salary and an average body. I can take care of myself, but...I'm lonely." Mona blurted, finally looking me in the eye.

That one glance confirmed my instincts were, as usual, spot on. There was strength in her, and grace as well. It was too bad she couldn't see it for herself; Mona Katz had a self-image problem, but her priorities were in the right place.

Most of the time, people hold *themselves* back from love—and they usually don't realize they're doing it.

Squeezing her into my packed schedule would require a shoehorn if I was going to take her on. I already knew I would. The force was strong with this one. Forgive the movie reference, but that's the best way to describe how I work. It's actually quite simple.

They talk, I listen, and eventually I get the buzz, the tingle. A tugging feeling that originates right behind my belly button, and if I follow the pull, it will lead me right to the perfect match. I'm almost never wrong. My friend and business partner, Flix, says I have an internal GPS, and it's always set to romance. I tell him he's being cheesy, but it's as good a description of my methods as any.

The average amount of time it takes me to locate a match is two hours—longer if I have to go outside the city. Mona's match was close. I could tell by the caliber of the sensation I was feeling. Really close, actually.

"...utter disaster when I found out he was still married." On a roll, Mona continued to tell me about the last time she had dated anyone.

In the early days, with a match this close, I would have dragged her out into the street to engineer a first meeting right there and then. I've learned a lot in the last few years. No one wants to believe true love is that easy to find. They expect more pomp. More circumstance. I've learned to give it to them.

"And he was cheating on both of us. It was devastating." I saw the ghosts of her sorrow reflected in

Mona's eyes. She hadn't just been beaten up by love; she had been burned, stomped into the ground, and then buried.

A boost of confidence is exactly what this woman needed, and I was more than prepared to give it to her.

I leaned back in my chair and looked at her thoughtfully for a moment, deciding that directness was the best option in this situation. "Mona, please don't take this the wrong way, but I think maybe you aren't giving yourself enough credit. You're a smart, attractive woman—don't roll your eyes, it's true—but you have to believe that for yourself if you want someone else to see you that way. Will you trust me to help you?"

She nodded hesitantly, and I went back over to my desk, pressed a button mounted beneath it, and marched over to a door in the corner most people assume opens into a closet. And while technically they're correct, this isn't where I keep my magic broom.

Indicating for Mona to follow me, I led her down a short hallway and into a large room, then spun around quickly to observe her reaction—this was my favorite part.

Incredulity and delight vied for first place as her gaze bounced from the racks of clothing and accessories to the Wall of Shoes, as I liked to call it, and finally lit on a stunning man leaning against a barber's chair and wielding a pair of gleaming gold scissors in his manicured fingertips.

Flix was pure manly perfection, personified, and he knew it. To regular humans who could not see past the glamour to his true face, he resembled a Greek god. Apollo or Adonis, too beautiful to be real. It was a damn shame the faeries on his mother's side of the family considered him an ugly duckling.

And if he was ugly, what order of magnitude would be considered handsome? Probably too much hotness to handle. But I will admit I'm curious. Who wouldn't be?

Being only half of something was one of our common threads; Flix was half faerie and half human, and I was half human and half witch—which made neither of us one thing or the other. We also both loved old movies, the more chick-flicky the better.

Still, I was pretty attached to the whisper of power I did have and had wished to be a real witch on every star in the sky, plus twenty-four years of birthday candles, and about a thousand stray eyelashes. Meanwhile, Flix, who had magic in spades but no higher purpose to use it, would have done anything to be a regular human.

"And what do we have here?" His melodic voice exaggerated for effect, rang out. "A beautiful Goddess, somewhere underneath all this..." he waved a hand theatrically and grimaced, "frump. Sit down, my love, and let me work my magic." Any hope Mona might have had for a match between Flix and herself was dashed as it became clear that his tendencies leaned in the opposite direction.

Mona quietly accepted her fate and spent a solid hour chewing on the inside of her lip as Flix yanked unapologetically at her hair, painting strands into individual squares of aluminum foil and applying several colors of dye. While that was setting, he turned his attention to her face. With gentle hands, he applied soothing balms and makeup of his own creation before combing, cutting, and teasing Mona's hair into submission.

While she was being poked and prodded, we learned that Mona was actually quite an accomplished pastry chef, and had recently taken a position at one of the best-kept secrets in town: Crumb, a bakery specializing in unique wedding and specialty cakes. We also learned that part of Mona's problem on dates might be that she didn't stop talking. Like, *ever*.

She told us about every dog she had owned since

the puppy she got on her fifth birthday. And then went on to provide exquisite detail about the last four wedding cakes she'd made.

I sensed the incessant chatter was a nervous habit and hoped getting her a little more comfortable in her own skin would give her that bit of confidence she seemed to need.

When Flix finally, with a flourish and a self-satisfied "Voila!", whirled her around to face the mirror Mona's mouth dropped open in disbelief.

Flix had worked with her natural hair color to create a dramatic multicolored effect, darker at the roots and fading subtly to golden blond at the ends. Layers framed her face, and long bangs swept across her forehead, enhancing her high cheekbones and bright blue eyes. Though he claimed not to use his magic on our clients, I sometimes wondered if he had a secret cache of faerie dust hidden in his apron pocket; but maybe he was just that good.

"I...I can't believe it." Mona breathed, looking back and forth between Flix and me as if wondering who to thank first.

"It has been my pleasure, my dear. All I did was make you look more like *you*. The natural beauty was there, it only needed to be released. Feeling good about your appearance has more to do with displaying who you are on the inside! Now, let's see what our Lexi can do about locating your soul mate."

Flix deposited a kiss on each of her cheeks, causing them to flush pink once more, and took his leave. With a noticeably lighter heart, Mona turned her head this way and that to get a good view in the mirror of what he had done.

"Does everyone get a makeover when they come here?" I could tell Mona was hoping she wasn't a special case and that this was just how things worked at FootSwept.

Putting people together was serious business, and the last thing I wanted was to make any of my clients think that finding a soul mate hinged on such superficial things as appearance. I firmly believe that love comes from the inside, not the outside. Let's face it, though. By the time most people get to me, they've been through the dating wringer, and a little pampering soothes the battle-weary soul.

"Everyone gets what they need." I hoped my answer was diplomatic enough. "Would you like to pick out something new to wear?"

"Is it part of the fee? I don't want charity." The vehemence in her voice suggested that she might have had to rely on the generosity of others in the past. "I have a great job. I can afford to pay."

I laid a hand on Mona's arm, "I'll let you in on a little secret. I have deals with nearly every clothing store in town. They give me a rock bottom discount price in exchange for sitting in on job interviews to give insights on which applicants will make the best employees. The clothes are part of the service, but it's up to you whether or not you want to choose an outfit."

When Mona hit my closet full of goodies, it was with a spring in her step. No woman could resist picking through that many pairs of boots.

"You hang onto those clothes for your date, and I'll work *my* magic. I'll call you in a few days, and we'll take the next step." I promised, sending her on her way and locking the door behind her. It was well past my official closing time, but I had no intention of heading home just yet, so I pressed the button under my desk again, and Flix appeared before me as if out of the ether.

"Glass of wine before you head for home?" He guessed and pulled a bottle of my favorite red out of his back pocket. "Or do you need a place to crash?" His affected accent was gone in the absence of paying clients, and he was back to being my regular old Flix. If you can call a sexy faerie man *regular* at all.

"An adamant *yes* to the former, and a regretful *no* to the latter. I'm going to have to bite it and see what havoc has been wreaked since I left this morning." Did I forget to mention that Flix isn't the only faerie in my life?

Most of my kind only have one faerie godmother—they're sort of like guardian angels for witches—but my sordid past had left me with three, and trust me, that's two too many. What's more, being sisters, they didn't always get along.

Witches rarely, if ever, meet their Fae benefactors and I was probably the first in history to live with one, though since the house we all occupied belonged to my grandmother, technically they lived with me. The four of us made an odd family, but it was the only family I'd ever known.

Hinting that I might be old enough to be on my own made them laugh, and not in such a nice way, either. I guess, compared to the few thousand they'd admit to, my paltry twenty-four years seemed about a minute long to the godmothers. Probably why they treated me like a child half the time.

Flix handed me a glass, and I swirled it around for a moment before taking a longer sip than necessary.

"With Vaeta back from the underworld, it's been a

little on the cray-cray side at my place. They've crammed a hundred years-worth of fighting into the span of six months, and they have no consideration for the fact that some of us need our beauty sleep."

If that sounded like envy, it wasn't. Much.

"I finally had to beg Terra to put a quiet charm on my bedroom."

Topping off my glass again, Flix quirked an eyebrow at my tone. "And how did that work out?"

"She made it so I can't hear anything at all when I'm in there; not my alarm, or my phone, or even my mp3 player. It's just completely silent now, which is even more annoying than the racket, and she won't lift the spell. But *I'm* the one acting childish?"

I ranted on while Flix finished off the bottle. "Not to mention, business has picked up exponentially lately. I'm even getting walk-ins these days."

"It's just a phase. In another month you'll go through a dry spell and be crying on my shoulder that no one needs you." An elegant shrug dismissed that worry, and Flix changed the subject back to the faeries.

"Vaeta still not fitting into the whole sister dynamic?"

He didn't seem surprised. We didn't talk much about his Fae heritage and I wondered if he identified with Vaeta since she was the household outcast at the moment. A feeling he knew well enough from interactions with his extended family.

"The other three think she's an idiot and are not shy about stating their opinion." That statement earned a raised eyebrow. We usually avoided the subject of his family, but what little he did say made me think they were a two-faced bunch of snobs. Sneaky with their condemnation of him and his status as a halfling.

Don't tell Flix, but there were times I would have traded a handful of sneaky faeries for the filter-free bunch I lived with.

"She's been in the underworld, I guess, for almost a hundred years. Lured by some demon with romance on his mind and poetry on his tongue, if Evian is to be believed. Vaeta is the romantic of the family."

Flix quirked a smile.

"Okay, romantic is the nicest word anyone has used. I believe the word nymphomaniac has come up a few times, but the upshot is that she ended up in hell because of a dude."

Is it ironic that half my business comes about because some woman has experienced that very same thing only metaphorically?

Absently flicking a finger to clean the wine glasses

and return them to the cabinet, Flix said, "I've heard my mother talk about that type of thing. Demons have a taste for Fae, and once on the hook, it's hard to get back out of the underworld."

My one and only brush with death occurred on the day Vaeta returned because she'd gone for the dramatics when setting up a reunion with her sisters.

"I'm not sure it was all that hard. She made her way into a nexus, lured and kidnapped a guardian angel to get the right mix of people there to open the portal, and then tripped out the door after tossing around a bunch of magic."

While I recounted the story for at least the third time, my fingers moved toward where my hairline arched over one eye. I touched the tiny scar where I'd hit my head on the edge of a mist-shrouded prison cell in the portal where Vaeta had made her stand.

Since her return, Flix hadn't been coming over as often.

"She says the demon was her captor, but all that time, her sisters thought she had chosen to turn her back on them. Which, I guess she kind of did, or she didn't realize she was in so deep until it was too late. Terra, Evian, and Soleil have been in my house for what feels like my entire life, and have literally never mentioned her. It's beyond strange that they could just pretend like she never existed. I mean, she's their sister, and I know it was painful, but...it seems cold."

Flix was silent for a long moment. "I imagine that kind of betrayal seems unthinkable to someone who has never experienced the way families can hurt one another."

I knew Flix's family wasn't the most loving, and if I could, I'd take all that pain away. It did irk that he seemed to have forgotten I knew exactly how easily families can hurt one another.

On that note, we closed up the shop and I headed home.

A Match Made in Spell is available now, or you can grab the box set of the first three books in the series at a discount. Keep reading for a preview of Murder Above the Fold.

EXCERPT FROM MURDER ABOVE THE FOLD

THE MAG AND CLARA BALEFIRE MYSTERIES - BOOK ONE

"Get your lazy butt out of bed, Clara Balefire. It was your idea to pick a peck of mugwort at the crack of dawn. Why I'm forced to act as your alarm clock when I've already brewed your coffee is beyond me." Mag's voice trailed off as she stomped back downstairs to the kitchen while Clara rolled her eyes, sighed, and attempted to yank the covers back over her head. Before she could drift back into dreamland, Pyewacket and Jinx pounced on top of her and let out a pair of yowls loud enough to wake the dead.

"I'll ban tuna from the house if you do that again." The familiars knew full well the threat was an empty one, and so they stepped up their game. Flashing into human form, they treated Clara to a duet in perfect harmony of "The Song That Doesn't End."

"All right, all right, I'm up." Clara's fuzzy-sock-clad feet hit the floor with a resounding thump, and with a snap of her fingers, she was dressed to start the day. "Shoo, you two."

When Clara finally descended the stairs, her sister was anxiously tapping her foot against scrubbed-to-gleaming oak floorboards, wearing an irritated expression on her deeply-lined face. Mag ignored Clara's blown raspberry, shoved a thermal mug of hazelnut-scented, caffeine-laden perfection and an empty basket into her hands, and the pair padded out onto the back porch.

"We'll have plenty of time; the sun hasn't even started to crest yet. You'll thank me next time one of your spells calls for mugwort dew, Miss Snarky Pants." Clara teased her sister.

Mag snorted. "There's a first time for everything."

Heaving an exaggerated sigh, Mag leaned more heavily on her cane than necessary, and followed Clara down a cobbled path leading toward the riverbank. When they'd scouted the property the previous winter, a recent thaw followed by a sudden re-freeze had pushed large chunks of broken ice far enough onto the shore that when spring arrived, and the water level returned to normal, it felt like the backyard had doubled in size.

The phenomenon had also disturbed the soil enough to create the perfect conditions for an abundant mugwort harvest, and Clara was determined to take advantage of the blessing. Being able to use the term "locally grown" in the ingredients list for her home-made products was an added bonus.

For all of Mag's griping, she enjoyed walking the trail between her new home and the town square. Not as much as she would enjoy a solo trip across the Andes lost in the wild thrill of the hunt, but that life was over. Time might heal most wounds, but never the ones of its own making, and if she had to be put out to pasture, Harmony's grass was as good as any.

"This is certainly a change, wouldn't you say?" Clara asked as they picked their way along the shore, every now and then finding a patch of feathery, dew-laden greens. With a snip of her shears, Clara clipped off some of the tender plants, shaking the beads of moisture into a wide-mouthed jar before adding the cuttings to the basket.

"I watched the suburbs swallow our home," she said as she sorted through to find the best shoots, "and I thought if I ever got back to myself again, I'd seen enough that it would be easy to acclimate. Twenty-five years frozen in time went by so slowly, but the world moved on, and I still feel like a walnut in an almond shell sometimes. Harmony seems like a nice enough place, and it's good to feel needed and vital after all those idle years."

"You know how I feel about crowds, Clarie," Mag replied. The use of her special pet name for her sister indicated she'd finally softened. "Still, maybe this little adventure of ours won't be so bad after all. I'll get to spend time with you, and watching Hagatha at work is anything but boring. I can see why the coven got tired of dealing with her." Mag accepted another handful of clippings from Clara and placed them in the basket.

"Can't say I blame them for that, but it's a shame nonetheless. I hope when we start to turn senile, we don't get tossed off like an old pair of shoes. Speaking of which..." Distracted by something she saw on the ground, Clara tripped, let out a grunt, and wound up on her backside covered in mugwort clippings, chestnut hair floating around her head in a disheveled halo.

Mag barked out a laugh, only sobering when she noted the expression of shocked consternation on her sister's face as she stared at a pair of shoes protruding from under a leafy bush.

For a fraction of a second, Mag wondered if either the glare from the rising sun or perhaps her old, tired eyes were playing tricks on her before resigning herself to the fact that there were, indeed, feet and legs attached to the shoes.

"I'm afraid we're not in Kansas anymore," Clara said, pushing herself up and taking a closer look at the feet that had tripped her. "Is that what I think it is?"

Clara nodded, "If you think it's a dead body, you'd be correct. What should we do?"

"Well, obviously you need to get out that blasted little contraption of yours and for once put it to good use. Call the cops. And don't touch anything. Forensics will want to sweep the area for trace evidence." Mag said knowingly. "It's procedure for unattended deaths."

Given the gravity of the situation, Clara resisted the urge to point out that Mag's closest dealings with a human forensics team came from her nightly obsession with police and crime shows. Instead, she pulled out her cell phone to do as her sister instructed.

"It's a woman, for sure, but I can't see her face from this angle." Mag crouched into a squat position worthy of the Yoga Journal, her injury forgotten and her cane left lying in the grass at her side. "It looks like she must have fallen and then rolled under there. See how none of the branches of this bush are bent or broken?" Mag pointed to the bridge towering overhead. "I didn't realize we'd come this far already. Tell them to take the footpath from the clock tower; we're not more than a stone's throw from the town square."

Clara relayed the necessary information, and to Mag's surprise, snapped a few photos of the grisly scene.

"What? If you weren't so tech-phobic, you'd be doing the same thing. Besides, you know you'll thank me later because if my intuition is screaming, yours must be whistling Dixie."

Using her cane for extra balance, Mag navigated the rocky hill to get to a position that revealed more of the body.

"Come here and look. I think I know who it is." Her voice held a note of sadness, and Clara scrambled up the bank to stand next to her sister. Leaves concealed the dead woman's face, and the terrain was too steep for them to bend over for a closer look without losing balance, so Clara snapped another series of photos before pocketing the phone.

Paisley cloth in colors now muted by mud and moss stains wrapped around thighs scraped by rough passage over sticks and stones. The bodice, barely visible below where the rest of the body disappeared into the glossy green foliage, was badly torn.

"You recognize that dress, don't you?" Mag asked gravely.

"I do," Clara replied. "Let's say the blessing for the dead, then leave her for the proper authorities, and we'd better make it the short version."

Together they chanted:

Gentle air carry her spirit home.

Mighty fire purify her soul.

Abiding water cleanse her pain.

Mother earth receive her heart.

Blessed be until the wheel returns thee.

Less than five minutes—which felt like at least fifty—later, a rustling noise signaled the approach of two men as they marched down the embankment to where the poor, dead woman lay. The younger of the two, a salt-and-pepper-haired man of about forty-five, clad in a police uniform, looked from Mag to Clara with a suspicious glint in his eyes.

"What were the two of you doing out here at this time of day? I don't know how they do things in the big city, but..." His beer belly jiggled over a large belt buckle in the shape of a ram's head. Neither Mag nor Clara got to hear exactly how things were done in a small town because the second man interrupted the interrogation with a wave of his hand.

"Chief Cobb, I think you can relax. See that basket? I believe these ladies are out here picking...some kind of weed." He reached out and pulled a piece of mugwort out of Clara's hair, his pleasant face turning bright red as his eyes met hers.

"I'm Mayor Norm McCreery, and I don't believe we've been properly introduced. You two recently purchased the old crow's house—I mean, Hagatha Crow's old house. Margaret and Clara Balefire, am I right?" As if Mag didn't exist, he directed his comments to Clara.

"Balefire," he said, tapping his chin and appraising the two women. "Interesting name. I apologize for Chief Cobb's lack of sensitivity. His people skills could use a little work. Ah, here's the EMT crew. Too bad it looks like it's too late for them to do anything."

As is the way of it in many small northeastern towns, people often wear several hats, and one of the emergency technicians conveniently served as the county coroner.

Treating Clara to a crooked smile, the mayor

rejoined a scowling Chief Cobb who had finished his preliminary examination and stepped aside to allow the coroner to move the body.

"If you ladies wouldn't mind taking a few steps back," the mayor said, "we'll need to ask you some questions as soon as we're done here."

"The chief is a bit brusque, but Mayor McCreery seems nice," Clara said in a tone low enough that only her sister could hear her.

"Mayor McCreepy if you ask me," Mag muttered under her breath.

"I don't know. He's handsome in that backwoods kind of way. Strikes me as the type of guy who owns a pair of red plaid flannel pajamas."

Mag rolled her eyes, "There's absolutely no reason for you to be imagining that man in his pajamas."

Clara jabbed her with an elbow. "That's not what I meant, and you know it. Get your mind out of the gutter and look—they're pulling her out." Clara jumped to her feet and stepped a few paces closer to the victim, Mag on her heels.

"We were right. It's Marsha from the newspaper office." Clara confirmed unnecessarily since Mag could see that clearly for herself.

The coroner squatted next to the body, looking back

over his shoulder to speak to Chief Cobb. "This head wound looks like the cause of death. I'd say she bounced off a rock somewhere before landing here. The preliminary estimate is she's been dead maybe twelve hours, a little less. Between ten and twelve. I'll know more when I get her on the table."

Ten or twelve hours would put the time of death between six and eight o'clock the night before. Just a few hours after the sisters had met Marsha for the first time.

"Seemed like such a nice woman," Clara whispered to Mag. "What a shame. I wonder if she fell, or if she... you know...jumped on purpose."

Mag drew her brows down and huffed. "Don't be stupid. Anyone who's serious about jumping off a bridge doesn't do it so close to the end. You want to die, you go right out into the middle where there's less chance of anything breaking your fall. Maximum velocity."

Clara looked at her like she'd lost her mind. "That's the most morbid thing you've ever said to me. Shh, he's coming back."

Mayor McCreery ambled back over to Mag and Clara. "I'm sorry you had to find her like this. Did you know Marsha Hutchins?"

"No." Clara replied, "I mean, we met her just yesterday at the newspaper office. She seemed nice. Do you know if she—"

"The guardrail on that bridge has been in need of repair since the Lester boys rammed it with their Jeep Wrangler last fall. It looks like Marsha must have been on her way home, stumbled and fell. She was known to take the footpath. Wouldn't be the first time someone has fallen—"

"Well, don't you think, Mr. *Mayor*, that you ought to do something about it?" Mag interrupted without mincing words. It didn't seem to matter to her that perhaps another time and place would have been more appropriate for a conversation about civic duties. Then again, Mag had never been fast friends with Miss Manners.

Mayor McCreery's face flushed a darker red than before. "Well, yes, you're probably right." He turned his attention back to Clara, obviously considering her the more reasonable of the pair. "I assure you, this was nothing more than a tragic accident, but the crime scene team from our county office will follow up. I do apologize. You and your mother have only been in town a few weeks, and I can't imagine how we compare to the way things are run in the city."

"Not at all, Mr. Mayor. Port Harbor isn't the thriving metropolis some people imagine it to be. I'm sure you'll do your due diligence."

"Clarie, I seem to be having another of my episodes," Mag's voice had gone from commanding to breathy in a matter of seconds, and she once again leaned heavily on her cane. Clara quirked an eyebrow but followed through with the necessary niceties before leading her sister slowly up the hill and into town.

Once they were out of sight of the mayor and police chief, Mag's strength returned full-force. "I'd bet my wand hand and a wad of Ben Franklins this was no accident. Couldn't you feel it?"

Clara nodded, glancing over her shoulder. "Something was definitely off, but we shouldn't jump to conclusions."

"I have no intention of jumping in any way, shape, or form. I intend to investigate, and you're going to help me." Mag marched ahead of Clara, who remained pensive as they ascended the hill and wove their way through a maze of gardens adjacent to the town office. Her absentminded admiration of a rainbow of budding tulips was rudely interrupted as the clock tower looming overhead rang out the seven o'clock hour.

"I'm glad we don't live right next door to that thing.

We'd both need hearing aids inside of a week. It's loud enough at the house as it is." Clara griped, sticking a finger in her ear and wiggling it around.

"What's that now?" Mag cupped her ear with one hand and grinned.

"You goof. Look, there's Leanne in the newspaper office." Clara pointed and dragged Mag across the grass and onto Main Street. Spurred by the desire to get as far away from the clock bells as possible, she set a brisk pace. "Should we go talk to her?"

Mag squared her shoulders as much as she could, anyway—they remained slightly hunched even when she stood upright—and led the way inside. "Hello, Leanne," she said to the young lady inside. "Do you remember us? I'm Mag, and this is my daughter, Clara."

"Sure, sure, come on in. Marsha should be here any minute. Maybe she slept in because we worked late finalizing the layout last night. Still, It's not like her to be tardy when there's a special edition in the works."

Clara and Mag exchanged a glance that included a silent conversation:

She doesn't know.

We're going to have to tell her.

You do it.

No, you do it.

Clara sighed; it was probably best for her to break the news. Gently, as the gravity of the situation warranted. "Leanne, I hate to have to tell you this, but Marsha won't be coming in today. She passed away last night."

Murder Above the Fold is available now.

OTHER BOOKS

If you'd like to meet more people who live rent-free in our heads, here's a list of other series we've written. Our books are all set in fictional towns in Maine, and some characters like to flit back and forth between series. The cast of Psychic Seasons hangs out with Everly and also with Lexi Balefire from the Fate Weaver series. Mag and Clara Balefire are Lexi's grandmother and aunt!

Psychic Seasons
Four women, four love stories, and a whole lot of supernatural surprises. In the quaint town of Oakville, Maine, psychic visions, ghostly whispers, and fate itself conspire to change lives—and hearts—forever

Haunted Everly After
Everly Dupree came home for a fresh start—not a full-time gig solving ghostly murders. But when the dearly

departed start demanding justice, what's a reluctant medium to do?

Ponderosa Pines Mysteries

Nothing bad ever happens in the weird little town of Ponderosa Pines...until someone dies. Now it's up to best friends Chloe and EV to solve the mystery—before the town's secrets bury them too.

Fate Weaver

Lexi Balefire—matchmaker, witch, and accidental fate-weaver—must balance love, magic, and a family legacy of chaos before destiny decides for her!

Mag and Clara Balefire Mysteries

Sister witches Mag and Clara Balefire move to a sleepy Maine town for a fresh start—only to find themselves conjuring up trouble, solving murders, and keeping their magic under wraps in this charmingly witchy cozy mystery series

Laurel Haven Witches

Four witches, destined by blood and magic, must embrace their power, battle a dark legacy, and surrender to the love that could break the curse—or bind them to it forever.

Nell Page: Accidental Investigator

Nell Page owns a bookstore, drinks too much coffee, and has a habit of noticing things she probably shouldn't. With warmth, wit, and an accidental talent for investigating, Nell tackles mysteries that don't always involve murder—but always matter.